Daisies

Jordan Shumate

Cover illustration by Madi Leigh

Dedicated to my family, who believed in me every
step of the way.

chapter 1:

My fingers move my pencil down repeatedly onto my desk in a steady rhythm, imitating the ticking of the clock in the far corner of the room. The fast beat distracts me, but it doesn't last as long as I hope.

The science classroom is eerily quiet today, however, I can tell that every student is itching to jump up and run out of this building. Upon closer inspection, I hear feet tapping lightly on the tile floors and see the fidgety movements of students as boredom sets in.

Student's eyes dart from their work to the clock every few seconds. Our teacher sits at her boring gray desk at the front of the classroom. The same one that sits in every single classroom at all of the public schools in our district. She is looking down at her laptop. It's the same one that is issued to all who come to teach at Stonebrook High.

Suddenly, she looks up from her work, trying to catch anyone not doing what they're supposed to, but we are all too fast. Being juniors at this school, we have mastered the art of escaping a teacher's icy, cold glare. I stare down at my piece of paper with just a few simple words on it, trying to focus on what I'm supposed to be doing instead of avoiding it any longer.

Write about a time that you have felt truly inspired.

This seems like a weird assignment for a science class, but that's what the first week of school is all about. Getting to know each other. We do the same things every year, introduce ourselves to all of our new teachers and classmates in all kinds of different ways. It seems like the school board has decided on a common theme for everyone to follow this year. I have already seen this request six times today: once in every one of my class periods, and I have basically made up my answers just to get through it each time.

I don't know why all of a sudden I am really trying to think deeply about it this time. Maybe it was seventh period delusion or the lack of sleep I got last night, but I really want to put effort into it this time. I shake my head to myself, ignoring these unusual thoughts and tell myself to just whiz through it again. I don't get the point in doing all of this anyway. But as I try to write, I can't seem to make my pencil move.

Write about a time that you have felt truly inspired.

I look in front of me to where Daisy Hayes is sitting, her bright red hair falling into a perfect pattern of ringlets on her back. Daisy and I have been friends since fifth grade and, although we have grown apart a little bit since then, I can always count on her as someone to entertain me during any of my classes. Not wanting to risk getting caught, I silently nudge my heeled boot into her calf and she whips her head around to face me.

"What?" she whispers, quietly, so that no one else but me can hear.

"I don't know what to write about," I answer simply. She rolls her eyes in response and I glance around her shoulder to see that her paper has scribbles written down the whole front side of it. I don't know how writing comes so easily to some people. That's not the case for me. I look back down to my page, empty, except for the flowers and hearts I doodled in the margins.

"What about that time you convinced Jeremy Shoemaker to eat twenty McDonald's hamburgers in 30 minutes and he did it without puking?" Daisy suggests and I raise my eyebrows at her. "What, don't give me that look, it was impressive!"

"Okay, one, I was trying to forget about that and two, how is that inspiring?"

She shrugs her shoulders at me. "I don't know, maybe you have an aspirational goal in life to eat twenty hamburgers in 30 minutes too?" she whispers.

"Yeah right," I sigh and roll my eyes, annoyed.

"Okay, okay I get it," she says while putting her hand up in the air, a signal she is backing off. She turns back to her work and I am left to my own thoughts again.

Someone's bubblegum pops and I check the clock again.

There are still thirty minutes left until I get to rush out of this dreadful building. There's one kid at a desk one row back and three seats to the left of me who is writing away, his pencil zooming across the paper. If only I could be like that.

I have never been one of those smart kids that gets straight A's in all of my classes. I'm sure my parents wished I could be, but it never seems to happen. I struggle with almost anything that has to do with academics in my life. I know that my parents are disappointed that they didn't get some sort of genius child, but I honestly don't care. Why should I care about grades when I have a social life to keep up with? I mean you can't seriously ask me to juggle all of my classwork and still manage to be at every party hosted this year, can you? That would be way too much effort for anyone, and high school is the time to have fun!

I shake my head quickly as I snap back to the present. I look back up at the clock. 3:40. Still twenty minutes left until the end of the school day. This clock seems like the slowest, dreariest clock in the entire school. I start to tap my foot on the hard floor, replacing the action of my pencil drumming. I am hoping that maybe, just maybe, this will speed that stupid clock up. I just wish there was some way school could go by faster.

After what seems like forever, the sweet, sweet sound of the seventh period bell fills my ears with joy. I am rushing to pack up my binder and notebook when Mrs. Rose, my science teacher, stops me in my tracks.

"Miss Bennett," she says in a serious tone. "Come see me at my desk please."

I spot Daisy waiting by the door and do a waving motion, signaling for her to leave, I'll catch up with her later.

Mrs. Rose is generally a nice teacher so I'm not too stressed about her request. Since I have had her as a science teacher all three years so far at Stonebrook, I know her pretty well.

I casually stride towards her desk, my backpack hanging by one strap over my right shoulder and a happy smile plastered on my face. My long blonde hair is swung over my left shoulder and falls in a perfect wavy pattern, stopping just below my shoulders. My ocean blue eyes perfectly match the golden eyeshadow that I am wearing today, which took more time than expected to do this morning.

As I stroll towards the front of the classroom, not even one worry passes through my head. I arrive at Mrs. Rose's desk and see that her face is less relaxed than usual, her lips pursed together and her eyebrows turned downward. Mrs. Rose looks flawless, even when she is stressed. She has short, brown curly hair that she wears in a bob and is always perfectly in place. Her cocoa tinted, silky smooth skin looks absolutely amazing today. I make a mental note to ask her about her skin routine later. I am about to say something when she beats me to it.

"Abigail, don't you think for even a second that I don't notice when you aren't paying attention in my class." The smile on my face quickly drops into a frown and my shoulders sink.

"Next time I catch you not doing what you are supposed to be doing, it will be a detention," she says sternly with a serious look on her face. Taken aback by her accusations I fall backwards a little bit, away from her desk.

"Excuse me?" I answer in a slightly annoyed tone.

"I said pay attention in my class or you will be spending your weekend in detention," she briefly repeats. Mrs. Rose is never like this. Something must be up with her, but I have more important things to do than dwell on my science teacher's mood. I quietly mutter a "Yes ma'am" and shuffle away, less confident than I was just a few seconds ago.

chapter 2:

Once I am in the crowded hallway, I rush to my locker, wanting to escape from that embarrassing moment. As I am about to leave, I see my best friend, Natalie, putting her binders away, two lockers down from mine. I slam my locker shut and walk over to her. She sees me almost immediately, and closes her locker as well to focus all of her attention on me. We quickly hug each other, as usual, and then I lean against a locker next to hers.

"I have something to tell you," we both say at the same time and then start to giggle.

"You first," I suggest, gesturing towards her.

"Alright! There's a party at Nate's house, nine o'clock tonight, to celebrate the first week of school."

"Oooh fun!" I exclaim. "Do you think you can give me a ride?"

"Sure! I'll be at your house at eight thirty, sound good?" Natalie asks.

I nod in response.

"Oh! And I said I would drive Daisy too, if that's okay with you?" she adds.

"Of course, you know I love Daisy!"

"Okay, it's your turn now," she presses.

I prepare to tell her about my encounter with Mrs. Rose but as I am about to speak, I see a puny freshman hustling down the hall towards us just a few feet away. I can tell the little girl is trying to avoid eye contact with all of us juniors. She is going as fast as she can and is keeping her eyes focused on her binder that she is carrying, wishing to be invisible.

Poor girl, I think to myself. She probably had a math class up here as there is one freshman classroom on this floor of the school. She has strawberry blonde hair with bangs that come down on her forehead. They're so low that you can barely see her eyes.

I nudge Natalie with my elbow and point down the hall towards the girl. We both exchange a sly grin and without thinking, stick our right feet out in front of us.

The freshman doesn't end up seeing our sandaled feet in time. As she trips and falls towards the tile floor, all of the binders that she is carrying fly out of her sweaty grip. She lands on the cold floor with a quiet "Umph", and struggles to gather up all of her belongings. A few of her papers have flown out and are strewn here and there throughout the corridor.

Everyone at their lockers take out their phones to snap a picture and burst into laughter while they turn their attention to the girl. She finally collects everything and walks away as fast as she can towards the door, sniffling. Her big brown eyes are staring down at her bright pink sneakers, as if they were the things that had wronged her.

As she sneaks a quick glance back at us, I think I see a thin tear roll down the side of her left cheek before she disappears.

Natalie and I head towards our buses together. I finish telling her about my close call with detention and wave goodbye as I climb up the stairs to my bus. As I sit down, I wonder what it must have been like for that little freshman, to be stuck in an unfamiliar place with people that only want to pick on you.

When I was a freshman, we were the oldest kids in the school and we still are. Our school is pretty new, and we are the first kids to experience it. I start to think about how sad that must have been for her, but I quickly brush it off.

Soon the bus reaches my stop and I jog home to complete some homework and get ready for tonight. I have a few butterflies in my stomach, which is an unusual feeling for me.

I can't explain it, but it makes me start to question whether or not I should go to the party tonight. *I should probably just stay at home and relax, you know, get an early start on some homework, go to bed early.*

Oh who am I kidding, of course I am not staying home! I'm probably just hungry. I brush off the sickness in my stomach and start rifling through my closet, trying to find the perfect outfit for tonight.

Ding! I glance over at my phone sitting on my bathroom counter. I have my hands poised above my head, trying to curl my hair in time for the party. It's a text from Natalie.

Natalie : Be there in ten!

I speedily finish up with my hair and turn off the curling iron. Grabbing my phone on the way out, I turn off the lights in my room and skip downstairs, heading through the kitchen.

"Aren't you a little overdressed to be staying home studying tonight?" I hear a serious tone say from behind me. It's my mom, catching me as I am about to head out the door. I stop dead in my tracks and turn around on my heel, only to meet an angry stare in my mother's eyes.

"Um, yeah about that-," I stutter, but stop when I see her face soften. I breathe a sigh of relief.

"I get it Abigail, I was young once too, I'm just joking," she says, giving me a much preferred warm smile. "Just please, don't let your social life get in the way of your grades or schoolwork."

I beam at her and nod to show that I understand. "Don't stress, it's just one night," I assure her. "And not to worry, I'll be home by eleven."

"You promise?" she confirms, holding out her pinky finger.

"I promise." I restate and intertwine my pinky with hers, sealing our deal. She pulls me in and gives me a tight bear hug.

"Mom! Come on!" I murmur into her chest.

"Okay, okay," she gives in, letting me go.

I continue rushing around the first story of our house, grabbing everything I need to bring with me.

"Bye, have fun!" Mom yells after me as I hurry towards the front door.

I twist my head over my shoulder and thank her before heading outside. I quickly spot Natalie's car sitting at the end of my driveway.

I jog over and open the passenger side door, ducking my head to get into the car. Once I shut the door behind me I look over at Natalie. She is wearing black jeans and a white cropped tank top along with a full face of makeup. I had settled earlier on an outfit very similar to hers, ripped blue jeans and a light pink crop top. I am going for a more innocent look with my light pink makeup and curled hair.

"Hey Abs!" she exclaims, her gaze falling towards me.

"Hi! You look amazing, as usual," I respond, referring to her ensemble. She immediately smiles wide.

"Aw, you do too, sweetie! Ready to go?" she questions.

"Yep! All set! We're picking up Daisy, right?" I confirm.

15

"Yeah, her house is close so we should be there soon," she

answers. As Natalie is backing up onto the street, I pull out my

phone to text Daisy that we are on the way. She replies saying that

she will be waiting outside for us when we get there.

"It's a nice night, isn't it?" Natalie mentions, making sure

there's no silence in the car.

"Yeah, it really is," I say, while looking out the window

and watching the rows of houses whir by us. The summer hasn't

truly ended yet so it's still light outside, even though it's almost

nine o'clock. The sky is clear, not a cloud to be seen, and I watch

the sun just dipping below the horizon in the distance.

"We're here!" Natalie chirps, startling me and awakening

me from my daze. I focus out the window again and I see Daisy

bounding towards us. She is wearing a white dress that suits her

perfectly. It is casual and flowy, perfect for tonight.

To my surprise, when she reaches us, she opens my door

instead of the one behind me. I give her a confused look and she

immediately starts talking.

"I'm sorry but I get car sick a lot, do you mind if I sit up here? Just for the ride there, you can have shotgun on the way back if you want?" she explains.

I smile at her, "Of course, I really don't mind," I say, unbuckling my seatbelt and moving to the second row of seats. Once I am back there I notice that Natalie has a few textbooks cluttering the passenger side seat, so I move to the left, behind the driver's seat and shut the door behind me.

Suddenly, Natalie turns the radio up to a very loud volume and yells, "C'mon girls, it's time to party!"

Daisy and I both look at Natalie jamming out while driving, bobbing her head and waving one hand in the air, moving to the music. We glance at each other and giggle, both knowing this is typical Natalie.

"Come on, is no one going to join me?!" Natalie screams over the deafening sound. Daisy and I meet each other's eyes and then start to dance along to the beat. We sing at the top of our lungs to our favorite songs and all end up in fits of laughter when they are over. I'm watching Daisy and Natalie having fun and getting lost in the music.

In a flash, everything changes.

The headlights come out of nowhere. Natalie screams and slams on the brakes. Horns blare. Everything starts to move in slow motion. Glass shatters.

The truck hits our passenger side, sending us rolling across the road. We stop on our side, sirens are flashing, I scream out for help.

I try to reach them: my friends. Natalie is not responding. Her head hangs limp, her seatbelt keeping her body in place. But she is breathing. She is okay. Everything is okay. *But Daisy, what about Daisy?*

I whip over to her. Blood on the white dress that just a few seconds ago had a happy life to live.

Daisy isn't breathing.

I cry and I cry. I scream and I yell. No one to help yet.

I become aware of the blinding pain in my head and legs.

The agony becomes too much and I too, soon black out, no

dreams, no memories, just nothing. A black abyss.

chapter 3:

When I wake up everything swirls around me. I am in a cold, small, glowing room. At first, I don't remember anything but then it all comes back to me in a flood of sights, sounds and emotions. I shake my head over and over again. *No, no, no, no , no, no. This can't be happening. It's not real, it's not real. It can't be real.* I hear the door open and I jump, scared of who it might be. My mom walks in and quietly shuts the door behind her. When she turns around and sees that I am conscious, her eyes widen and she rushes over to my side.

"Oh my gosh! You're awake! How are you feeling?" She puts on a smile but her intense worry shows through and a wave of guilt passes through me. She has dark purple bags under her eyes and her normally calm face is tense and stressed.

I just groan. I don't feel like doing or saying anything. I look down at my legs and see full casts around them. My eyes go big at the sight of the bandages and the room is quiet for a moment. I am in a light blue hospital gown and a white, fluffy blanket covers my skin, keeping me warm. A shooting pain goes through both of my legs and I whimper and flinch.

My mom's face turns soft. "I know, sweetie, you must be in a lot of pain right now, but I am so glad that you're finally awake, I'll get the nurses to check your vitals and then we can go see Dr. Smith."

"Who?" I ask, not really wanting to know.

"Dr. Smith. He's the one who's been taking care of you over the past week while you have been unconscious."

My mouth falls open in shock as I try to process this news.

"Week? I've been asleep for that long?"

"Yes, Abigail," my mother says. She stays quiet for a minute. I don't know what to do, everything causes me pain. It's silent for a few minutes, my mom sitting still at the edge of my bed while I pick at my fingers.

Then I remember something. *Natalie and Daisy.*

"Natalie and Daisy?" I mumble, still looking down.

"Hmm?" My mom requests.

"Where are Natalie and Daisy?" I yell, suddenly very angry. I think I know the answer, but I don't want to believe it. I can't let myself believe it.

"Natalie's here baby, just a couple of rooms down, only a minor concussion from hitting her head on the window. She's okay. They're planning on releasing her later today," my mom responds. But I know her, I know she's not telling me something.

"Daisy?" I question quietly. The room goes silent and I know. It was real. It wasn't a dream.

"Oh Abby I'm so sorry but she, sh-she um, passed away. She was killed u-u-upon impact with the t-t-truck," my mom stutters. I can see the tears in her eyes for a moment before every emotion in my body goes into overdrive.

"No, no, no!" I scream and cry, I thrash my arms around and try to move as much as I can. I can't accept that. I cannot. Sweet Daisy. She was my age. She was my friend. She couldn't have died. Hot tears are streaming down my face. I am still screaming and yelling out. My mom wraps her arms around my body trying to calm me down. I stop screaming and sob into her chest. She hushes me, stroking up and down my back causing me to breathe deeply, in and out.

Soon I stop crying, but it's not because I have calmed down, or that I have become at peace with what happened, it's because I have no tears left. I can't do anything, my whole body feels completely numb. A nurse comes in to check on me, and then they let me go to sleep.

When I wake up again, I think everything is a dream, but when I try to move to get out of bed, I am reminded of the painful truth. Daisy's gone, and I have both of my legs in casts.

My mom is sitting beside my bed and when she hears me rustling her head snaps up from her magazine. She moves quickly and swiftly over to me. She is checking my temperature and holding my face in her hands. Normally I would shake her off, but right now I don't have enough energy to care. Once she has completed her check up, she moves towards the door.

"I'm going to go get a nurse to come in here. She will help you get strapped up in your wheelchair and…"

"Wheelchair?!?!" I interrupt. This revelation startles me enough to bring back a little bit of my energy. I am in shock. I mean, I guess there isn't another way for me to get around. I just never thought that *I* would be in a wheelchair.

"Mhmm," she hums as a yes. "That's why we are going to see Dr. Smith. He is going to estimate how long you have to be in that bad boy." She gestures behind her using her thumb and chuckles. I can tell she is trying to use a little humor to lighten up the room, but I'm not in the mood.

There it is. *My* wheelchair. Sitting there all pristine and shiny in the corner of the room. I don't understand why this is happening to me. I just want to go back to sleep and not wake up again until this all proves to be a nightmare.

A nurse comes in and does all of the routine poking and prodding on my skin, checking to make sure I am stable enough to get out of my room for a couple of hours. She carries me out of my hospital bed. I try to struggle but eventually give up, powerless and defeated.

She carefully sets me down in the black wheelchair and then pats my shoulder, signaling I am all set and ready to go.

"Comfy?" she asks. I am definitely not comfy, but I lie and give a small nod anyway. Mom pushes me from behind, wheeling me down the cold, dimly lit corridor. I hear her say a quick goodbye and thank you to the nurse as we leave the comfort of my room.

Shivers run down my spine as I take in the sight. The hallway ahead of me is cold and bleak, like a never ending prison cell. The lack of sun and the dropping temperature makes the short walk seem like a dreaded march to my death, although I guess I'm not exactly marching.

We are the only ones in the corridor and my wheel chair squeaks a little too loudly. I look down at my hands and play with my fingers, trying to avoid looking up and feeling my stomach drop to the floor.

After a few seconds, the squeaking stops and I look up. There is a dark wooden door with a silver plaque that reads "Dr. Andrew Smith." God, what a generic name. I can already tell I won't like this guy, and I haven't even met him yet.

"You ready?" my mom whispers.

"Sure," I answer with a slight nod. I don't have the strength to do anything. I simply want to go home, to wake up from this sick nightmare. My legs are starting to hurt again and I just want to get this over with. The door opens with a slight creak and I see a desk with important looking papers strewn everywhere.

"Ahh, Abigail. Come in, come in. Sorry for the mess," says a man that I understand to be Dr. Smith. He is standing behind the desk and is trying to mesh all of the papers into a single pile, but his efforts are failing. He is wearing a white lab coat and thick, black framed glasses over his green eyes. His short, caramel colored hair is messy, as if he has run his hands through it one too many times today.

I take a closer look at his desk and see a picture in a silver frame. It has what looks like a younger version of Dr. Smith, wearing a goofy smile and slinging his arm around a young woman with blue eyes and straight black hair. In front of them are two young children who look to be about four or five years old. They both have greenish eyes just like Dr. Smith. One is a girl with long, straight jet black hair, like her mom and one a boy, with short, messy brown hair, just like his dad.

"Oh, it's fine. Don't worry about it," Mom says, interrupting my train of thought. As she says this, she waves away the subject with a quick gesture of her hand, motioning that it's no big deal. I would have to disagree. This place is a disaster.

"What have you found out about Abigail?" Mom questions, eager to get to the point.

"Well, this case is much, much, worse than I had originally perceived it to be," Dr. Smith says, suddenly becoming serious. My palms, which are already sweaty, start to grow even more clammy and I look down at the floor. I bite my lip out of anxiety and nervousness.

"I am going to make this quick and simple. Like ripping off a band aid," he says, gesturing towards me. "Abigail…"

I look up and meet his eyes.

"Yes?" I answer in a meek voice. I sound like a small child and I hate it. I don't like seeming weak, but I can't help it in this situation.

He takes a deep breath in, like he is preparing himself for the news he doesn't want to give. I see the sullen look in his eyes and know, before he even says anything, that this is not the good announcement I was hoping for.

He gives up on stalling and lets out a heavy sigh. "You may be stuck in that wheelchair for the rest of your life."

chapter 4:

My eyes go wide with fear and I immediately feel dizzy.
The room starts to spin as my brain tries to process what I have
just been told. My mom starts to quietly cry in the background
but I am too shocked to do anything.

Pain shoots through my body in quick waves. I blink my
eyes rapidly, hoping this is all a dream or some crazy prank, but
deep down, I know it isn't. My body, trying to cope with the
shock, starts to tremble, but not enough for anyone else to notice.

Dr. Smith looks down at his clipboard that he must have
picked up when I was distracted.

Tears well up in my eyes. I try to push myself away. Away
from the doctor, away from my mother, away from this harsh
reality that I now have to face, but Mom tightens her grip, letting
me know that I am not going anywhere.

"But-but-but-" I stammer. The expression on my face is
one I have never made before, caused by such strong emotions I

have never felt in my life. Shock, sadness, and exhaustion all combined into one horrifying look. Mom has an expression on her face that I assume resembles mine, as she looks exactly the way I feel.

"I'm so, so sorry Abigail," Dr. Smith whispers. "We can always try for improvement but I'm not sure there's much I can do."

"NO! NO! NO!" I yell at him, more angry than sad. "I refuse to believe that you, a life saving doctor, can't fix me!"

His face is still calm. "There is nothing within you to fix. Just some changes in the script of life to adjust to. You'll just have more challenges than-"

"*Just some changes in the script of life,*" I mock in a high pitched tone. "Whatever. I'm out of here." I finally break free of my mom and move myself back down the corridor. My arms burn like fire from pushing my new wheelchair so rapidly but I keep going. Big fat tears stream down my face as I race towards the sign with the word "Restroom" painted on it. It's the only safe place that I can think of.

I finally reach the white swinging door that reads "Women" and shove my way in, which proves to be difficult in my current situation. I can hear my mom's feet bouncing off the floor as she runs after me, not very far behind. I manage to shove the door open, quickly wheel inside, slam the door shut and turn the lock before she gets to me.

Just a couple of days ago, my biggest worry was how I looked in the morning or what I wanted for breakfast, but now everything has completely changed. I have bigger problems than cereal on my hands. I can't believe that I am here. A night that was supposed to be full of fun had turned into a complete nightmare. I may have just ruined my life forever. I shouldn't have ignored my gut. I should have stayed home.

My mom continuously knocks on the door, trying to get through to me. I just stare at the bare walls of the restroom and sit silently. I can't say anything because of the fear that I will make my situation even worse. Suddenly, the knocking stops and I hear my mom's fragile body slide down the door. Small, quiet sobs come out of her mouth, and even though she's trying to not let me hear her, I still catch it.

A wave of guilt washes over me and makes my heart hurt with sadness. With all of the commotion, I have been too selfish to think of how this might impact her. I am her only daughter, her eldest child. I am her life, she might even feel worse than me right now.

Slowly I unlock the door and open it slightly, peering at my mom through the crack.

"Hi," I manage to squeak out. My face is red and puffy from all of the crying and I have a major headache. She quickly scurries to stand up and face me.

"Hey," she responds. I open the door, little by little until I am sitting directly in front of her. The dark bags under her eyes have gotten worse since I last saw her and the rest of her face looks like mine: puffy, red and sad.

"I just texted Dad, saying that you are awake, he's on his way," my mom says, trying to avoid looking me in the eye. "Oh, and Alex is coming too, he can't wait to see his big sister. According to your father, he is jumping up and down in the car with excitement." She chuckles at the last part and a small smile creeps onto my face as I think about my dad driving our small minivan and Alex bouncing in the back seat. My Dad must be going crazy.

Alex is only eleven years old and is so full of energy, he drives us all mad, but I still don't know what I would do without him. He is only going into sixth grade but he is already an athletic prodigy. He plays basketball, baseball, flag football, and even lacrosse, but his main sport that he absolutely loves is soccer. That eleven year old boy can beat anyone in a soccer match and can easily outrun me. Thinking of Alex makes me feel the happiest I have been in the past hour, and it feels wonderful, like a huge weight has been lifted off of my shoulders.

"Sounds good," I reply, still grinning. A warm feeling ripples through my body as I think about what seeing my family will be like. I feel like I haven't seen them in so long, even though it's only been a week.

"It's nice to see you like this," Mom says, acknowledging my smile. "I feel like I have my baby girl back." She leans down and hugs me, and for a moment, I forget all of my pain and let my troubles slip away.

chapter 5:

Mom helps me wheel back to my hospital room so that I can wait for the rest of my family to arrive. I eat a grilled cheese sandwich while I wait, and life starts to feel a little more like normal,, you know, besides never being able to walk again.

When Alex and Dad enter the room, a smile immediately spreads across my face. Alex shuffles in, lifting a big teddy bear, bigger than him in front of his face. He peers around the huge head of the teddy bear and sees me. Dragging the bear behind him, he runs over to my bed, grinning with glee.

"Abby!" he yells while jumping onto my bed. His energy and excitement make me forget all about my injuries. The joy in his eyes is something I know I will never forget.

"What's up buddy? How's school?" I ask, ruffling his hair as he bounces gleefully in front of me. He is so full of energy, he looks like he might burst.

"Oh, well, it's okay I guess," he responds, while glancing down at my legs. This is clearly not the topic that he wants to discuss. "What are those big things on your feet?" he wonders aloud, pointing to my casts and getting sidetracked.

"Oh, they're casts, they help my legs heal by keeping my bones in place. Did Dad tell you what happened?"

"Yeah, he told me. A big, scary truck crashed into you, right?" His eyes are full of wonder and mystery. I chuckle at his description of the "big, scary, truck" but I let it go and answer his question.

"Right," I confirm with a small nod. Alex looks down silently, as he thinks of something else to say. Suddenly, his head bobs up and his face brightens. He pulls the teddy bear out from behind his back and shoves it into my lap. I notice something tied around the bear that I didn't notice before. There is a white envelope, attached to the bear's neck, that practically glows in the flourescent light of my hospital room

"For you!" he exclaims while pointing to the bear.

"Thanks Buddy!" I say and mess up his hair again. The room grows calmingly silent as I carefully untie the ribbon and look at the letter. My name is written in messy letters that can only be my little brother's writing. I open the letter and attempt to read what Alex has written, but it's a bit of a challenge. It takes me a while, but I am finally able to decipher his handwriting.

Dear Abigail,

I am so sorry that you got hurt. Me and Daddy really miss you. I hope you're okay and feeling better soon so that you can come home and everything can go back to normal.

Love, Alex

I glance up from the letter with tears filling my eyes and see Alex waiting expectantly at the foot of my bed. I lean towards him and give him a big hug.

"Thank you Alex," I say and a happy smile greets me in return. I hug him one last time before turning my attention to my dad.

He is still standing by the door and is holding a bouquet of flowers in one hand and has a box of chocolates in the other. He is normally a strong, tough-guy type of man, but when he sees me, his eyes well up with tears. He rushes over to hug me on my bed where I am sitting and embraces me with nothing but warmth and love. I wish I never have to leave his arms, I feel safe here, protected from all of the evils of the world. I sit there for a few moments savoring the feeling.

"Dadda?" I whisper. I haven't called him that since I decided I was too old for it in sixth grade.

"Yes baby girl," he answers. I can tell by the tone of his voice that he will tell me anything I want him to.

"What's going to happen to me?" I say, tears starting to flood my eyes again.

"I don't know baby girl, I don't know. But I do know one thing, us Bennetts, we never go down without a good fight.

chapter 6:

That night my family goes back home, and the next morning, Mom leaves as well. I can tell that she really needs some time at home, mainly to shower and get a change of clothes. I know that any time she spends away from me, even if it is just an hour, she will spend worrying, but she has to take some alone time.

Every few minutes, I can hear a distant phone ringing or some voices in the hallway, but other than that, everything in the hospital is quiet.

I pull out my favorite book, *Little Women* by Louisa May Alcott, from the backpack that my mom brought back with her after the last time she went home, when I was still unconscious.

I unfold the page that I had stopped on the last day I was in school. I am only a few pages in but I have read this book so many times that I know how the whole story plays out. The spine of the book is wrinkled and has white creases running up and down the side. The cover is worn and faded from the many

challenges it has withstood. It has been dropped in puddles,

buried in sand, even chewed on by a few dogs, but to me, it is the

most beautiful thing I own.

From the first time I laid my eyes on it when I was just

six, to this day, at seventeen years old, it has been precious to me,

one of the only things that is truly mine. In my head, I could

relate to all of the March sisters in different ways. *Little Women* has

always really resonated with me. I have read this book over and

over again, so many times that I can recite the whole first five

chapters by heart.

I look down at the antique book in my hands then slam it

shut. Tears start to well up in my eyes. The last time I was reading

this, I had such a perfect, normal life. That has all been taken

from me now.

Suddenly, I am filled with an anger and rage that I have

never seen in myself before. I am mad at everything, my mom, my dad, Alex, and most of all, Natalie. This somehow just became all their fault.

It is their fault I got hurt, their fault I am miserable, their fault my whole life is now ruined! Natalie pressured me into going to that party with her that night. My parents were the ones who didn't care. Who let me go to a party on a Monday night! Who does that? I should've known something would happen. I shouldn't have ignored my gut.

With a blazing fire in my eyes, I hurl my book across the room with outrage so fierce, I swear my whole face is on fire. It slingshots off of the wall with a sharp smack and I snap out of my temper.

My eyes go wide and I slowly bring my hands up to my mouth as I realize what I have just done. I start to quietly sob to myself. I can't remember what just happened, it's all foggy in my mind, I just recall being filled to the brim with frustration.

A nurse cautiously comes into my room to check on what the commotion is.

I lie and tell her that I just dropped my book and that it is no big deal. I don't need another person thinking that I am crazy.

She gives me a weird look, like she doesn't quite believe me. The room is silent for a few moments more, before I guess she decides it's not her battle and gives up. Since she is in my room already, she says she's just going to give me a quick checkup and I follow along obediently.

She does a few tests, then walks back out into the hallway, but not without a skeptical glance behind her. I smile and wave pleasantly, reassuring her that everything is fine.

Once she is gone, l am left to be alone with my thoughts. I don't know what just happened. It all went by in a blur, like my brain couldn't catch up with my emotions. I need to figure this out.

I don't have very much time to think about it before my mom comes back to the hospital. Dad and Alex stay home this time, but my mom walks in with a little more pep in her step.

She still has a fake smile planted on her face, although it is more genuine than before she left this morning, and it looks like she finally got a couple hours of sleep. I am beyond happy to have someone here with me and to see that her time at home did her well. However, I also wish I could've had more time to contemplate the little tantrum I had just a short time ago. Since then, nurses have come in to check on me every few minutes or so, throwing suspicious glances my way.

My mom comes in and sits on the foot of my bed. Everything is quiet for a few moments before yet another nurse strolls in casually.

"Is anything wrong?" my mom asks the nurse, coming to my rescue with a mischievous twinkle in her eyes.

"Um… No ma'am, everything is fine," responds the young man, obviously nervous of being caught. He must have not seen my mom walk in a few seconds ago. He is a phony, just like everyone else here. It seems as though everyone who works in this hospital are just here to mock their patients, while all of the people like me are stuck in a hopeless daze.

I snap out of my train of thought and look back to my mom. She is staring at me intently with wide eyes, studying me. I lean back a little, startled by the look she is giving me.

"Mom!" I yell, jokingly mad at her. I scowl at her playfully and she laughs.

"Sorry honey," she apologizes. "I'm just trying to figure out why you seem so confused."

"Oh it's nothing," I respond. She looks at me quizzically, her eyebrows turned down and her face puzzled.

"I swear! It's nothing for you to worry about!" I yell, only slightly annoyed at her pestering.

"Okay, okay!" my mom says, chuckling and putting her hands up in the air in defeat.

"Teenagers," she then sighs under her breath. I act like I don't hear her and stare down at my hands. The room becomes still for a few seconds.

"So…" my mom breathes, breaking the silence. "What did you do while I was gone?" She is trying to make conversation. As the days go on, we spend more and more time together and we are pretty much out of things to talk about. She knows everything about me, and vice versa.

"Well," I start. "I read for a couple of minutes but mostly just slept the whole time. I'm still really exhausted." I don't want to tell her quite yet about my explosion of anger. Same as with the nurse, I don't want to seem crazy, especially when I might get to go home soon.

"Good, good. It's perfectly fine to get your rest sweetie."

The room goes hushed again as we have run out of stuff to say. All is calm in this little hospital room that has become my world over the past few days.

All of a sudden, my room of peacefulness abruptly turns into a world full of burning pain as jarring shocks surge up from my legs and electrify my whole body. The doctor said it would be

46

common to have attacks like this for the first few weeks. I guess this is my first one.

I can't see anything because my eyes have automatically started to squint shut, almost like a reflex from my body trying to get rid of the agony. My legs whip violently back and forth under my sheets. I don't know what is happening. I don't know what to do. I can't think straight, I can't see straight, I can't hear straight.

A piercing scream cuts through the air, and it takes me a couple of seconds to realize it is coming out of my own mouth.

Nurses rush in to crowd around me and I hear all of the orders being shouted from every direction. The sounds all blare in my ears and fill my senses with confusion and irritation. I start to get dizzy and my head starts to pound like a drum. Everything is so overwhelming, it doesn't seem real.

"Why me?!" I cry out in anguish. I know everybody in the room must have heard me but there is too much chaos to focus on my voice. The last thing I see is my mom; she is leaning over the railing of my bed and stroking my head appeasingly with eyes so scared, I think she might collapse, right here on the spot.

"It's going to be okay, sweetie," she whispers into my ear. "Everything's going to be fine." I relax with her words and let myself sink into the bed and lay still, the fire still raging through my body, but the least I can do is try to save my mom from the torment she must feel seeing me in anguish.

And then, as suddenly as it came, the pain is gone. Everything stands still in my head but the mayhem is still continuing around me. People rushing for medications and nurses checking my pulse for any abnormalities.

"Everyone, stop!" I yell. Everything in the room comes to a halt at my command. Questioning stares wash over everyone's faces, all directed at me. My mom gawks at me blankly, wondering what is going on. I open my mouth to start to explain but I don't get a chance before a thermometer is shoved under my tongue. I push back the woman holding it and spit the tool furiously out of my mouth.

"It's okay! I feel better now. No more pain," I say, throwing my hands up in the air, exasperated. A chorus of complaints fills the air.

"Are you sure?"

"You don't seem okay!"

"You were screaming just a second ago."

"You can't be fine, it's impossible."

I want to yell. I am so sick of everybody here not taking me seriously.

"Don't you think I know my body better than you guys do?" I ask loudly. All other voices diminish. "I know how I'm feeling, and I'm feeling perfectly fine!" I argue. Everyone looks around at each other guiltily and ashamed. I don't think they enjoy being yelled at by a seventeen year old but they know that I'm right.

"Now. Listen. To. Me. I. Am. Fine!" I say, making sure to annunciate all of my words so that these people finally understand me.

49

Everyone starts to trickle out of the room, but not before making all of their final checks, nudging and jostling me until I convince them to leave. Now the only person left is my mom, and I think I am ready to talk to her.

chapter 7:

I need to tell my mom about what happened while she was gone. I need someone to consult with, someone who might understand what I am going through, but before I can even open my mouth to speak, she starts talking.

"Sweetheart, I'm not trying to be rude, but are you sure you're okay?" She still looks at me with wonder in her eyes but that is to be expected. I don't even know how the pain went away so quickly, but I really wish that people would stop asking me that.

I roll my eyes at her, annoyed. I know it's rude but I can't help it. She flinches and looks down at her lap as my actions poke a little hole in her heart. I feel sorry at once. It's a mother's job to look after her children, and I know that my mom is just trying to fulfill her duty.

"Yes, I'm fine," I whisper with as much sweetness in my voice as I can stand. I am trying to make her feel better by comforting and reassuring her. She looks up into my eyes and gives me the smallest smile, so tiny, it is hard to tell that it is there.

The silence has crept back into the room, but this time, it isn't awkward or painful, but compassionate and caring, like a blanket.

I don't dare to break up this moment until I know that it has gone on for long enough. After about two minutes, I speak up.

"Mom?" My voice is quiet and meek, like a little child's. I still don't like how weak I sound, but I don't really have a choice.

She looks a bit startled by my talking but then relaxes, letting the muscles in her face loosen. I didn't realized that she was so tense. Knowing that I have her attention, I continue.

"I have something to tell you." I blurt out quickly.

Immediately, she goes into protective mom mode, her eyes darting around the room for any sign of danger.

"It's okay," I say, soothingly. "It's nothing to worry about." She stops freaking out and her eyes settle on my face. She takes deep breaths to calm herself down and then quiets, waiting for me to talk.

"It's no big deal," I start. "It's just, a little bit ago, while you were gone, something happened." I stop to make sure she is listening and she nods, eager for me to continue.

"Earlier, I picked up my book to start reading, thinking that it would calm my mind down and give me a sense of comfort. Soon after, I ended up thinking a lot about home, and how different my life was before- well you know," I hesitate, not wanting to think of the crash.

"The incident?" she adds, wondering if that's what I am thinking of.

"Sure," I say. "Yeah, yeah the incident. Anyway, I was thinking about how normal my life was and how perfect everything would be if none of this would have happened and suddenly, I was filled with rage, I even threw my book across the room, chucking it into the wall." She looks at me quizzically, trying to put together everything that I am saying.

I finish my story and tell her everything about the nurses all the way up until she got here. When I finish, she stays hushed for a minute, gazing up at the ceiling.

"Here's what I'm thinking," she finally says, although she does not look down at me. "I think that you had a breakdown because you miss your old life. You miss the convenience, the normalness, the luxury of everything before the accident. And you are either angry at yourself for not knowing the real value of your old life before it was taken away, or you're mad at the world for taking it away from you."

She finishes and drops her eyes down to be level with mine. I think about her response for a minute. I understand everything that she had just said, and yet, none of it makes sense.

If I am so angry about the way my life is now, how come I'm not mad as I am sitting here? As far as I can tell, I still have two broken legs and my old life is still as far away as it was this morning.

I am so confused. I comb my hand through my matted hair, stressing myself over a simple answer to a question I had asked in the first place. My eyes drift to the cold white ceiling as I wonder, *Why, why, why is my life so complicated?*

After what seems like forever, my mom quietly stands up to leave, I open my mouth in objection but she silences me by lightly pushing my head back down into my pillow. As my body hits down on the soft bed, I realize that for some inexplicable reason, I am really tired. Before Mom even leaves the room, my eyes heavily droop shut and I lie, curled up on the hospital bed, asleep.

One of our favorite songs is playing. Natalie and Daisy are dancing in the front seat. Everyone seems happy. But something feels off. In a flash, the fun ends. There is blood everywhere. Pain everywhere. I am lifted into an ambulance, sirens wailing all around me. I can hear my mom screaming in the background. "No! You don't understand! I need to be with my daughter! She needs me! No, please no!" I try to lift my head to see her, but a surge of pain

sends me back into a haze. "Abigail! Abigail can you hear me! Abigail!"

chapter 8:

"Abigail! Abigail! Wake up sweetheart! We're meeting with Dr. Smith again today!" I open my eyes in a groggy daze. I sit up to look at my mom and find her standing at the edge of my bed, rubbing my legs. I groan and fall back down into my pillow. I'm even more tired now than I was before I fell asleep. I look at the clock next to my bed, it's already ten in the morning.

"Oh come on honey, you have to wake up! Did you hear me? I said, we have to go meet Dr. Smith!" This time she says it a bit louder, but I heard her the first time, I just didn't want to respond. I hate that my doctor's last name is Smith. It's just so universal and boring.

"But, Mom," I whine, dragging out my words and acting like an annoying three year old.

"Don't 'but, Mom' me! We have to go soon. I talked to one of the nurses and she said that there is a rumor going around that you might get to go home today! Isn't that good news?"

I don't really know if that's good news. On one hand, I'll get to go home and sleep in my own bed. Things will be back to normal or I guess as close to normal that they can be. And, that also means that I will have to go back to school soon, probably within the next week or so. But on the other hand, I'm a little bit scared to re-insert myself back into the real world.

I am soon dragged out of bed, in spite of my continuous protests, and helped into my wheelchair. It's easier to get around now than a few days ago.

I am wheeled through the same hallways as before, but I am so tired, everything passes by in a blur.

My mom knocks on the same dark wooden door and I think back to the last time I was here. That feels like it was centuries ago.

At first, no one answers the door. I am immediately filled with a rush of joy, glad to avoid the situation in any way possible, but then, to my dismay, my mom knocks again.

This time, we hear a loud thump against the door and my mom stumbles backwards. Dr. Smith opens the door slowly, inch by inch.

"Um, hello," he mumbles. Seriously, out of all the doctors in the state, my mom had to pick this one. Dr. Smith acts like a scared little child, he is messy, quiet, and uncertain. Not confident, assuring, and brave like a doctor should be. Even his hello sounds like a question.

When my mom and I peek past him into his 'office' we see that it is even more muddled than it was the last time we were in here, and that's saying a lot. I am personally shocked by the chaos and I see a similar emotion on my mom's face.

Seeing the appalled expressions we are both wearing, he adds, "Sorry for the mess again. I have had a lot of work to do recently." He glances at me and I immediately feel guilty, although this is probably not my doing alone.

Dr. Smith moves out of the doorway and my mom and I try to navigate my wheelchair into the room. It takes some time but eventually we are sitting in front of the doctor, awaiting the news we came here for.

"So, first thing's first," he says, turning to face me.

"How are you doing Abigail?"

"Uhhhh, okay I guess," I murmur, not looking him in the eyes. I don't feel comfortable in here, it's just so tense.

"I know that it's a lot to get used to at first, but you'll be fine." He doesn't really seem to care about the small talk and silence hangs in the air for a few seconds before someone speaks again.

"Anyway," my mom starts. "We were wondering whether or not Abigail could come home? We spoke earlier, remember?"

"Ah, ah, yes, I remember." he stutters. "Well, I have spoken to some of the nurses, and according to their observations, you will be able to go home as soon as possible, maybe as quickly as tonight."

I don't want to seem overeager but I can't restrain the giddy smile that spreads across my face. My heart lightens with this news. Going home means that everything will be going back to the usual soon. I will be able to be a typical teenager again, except for one thing, I'll still be in a wheelchair. I'm not complaining though, being in a wheelchair is much better than being in a hospital.

My mom lets a sigh of relief escape from her lips and leans down to plant a small kiss on the top of my head. Dr. Smith smiles a bit as well, happy to see his patients joyful, though he still looks wary.

We go through a few more details with the doctors before I can leave. Things like painkillers I can take and how to navigate around the house while still not being able to walk. My thoughts are elsewhere though, thinking of the paradise I will be able to experience once I am at home.

The little things such as reading a new book, or sleeping in my own bed seem like a luxury. Even going to school and seeing my friends seems like so long ago. My mind flutters to a picture of me laying on my fluffy blanket relaxing…

"Abigail?" My mom says expectantly, snapping me out of my daydream.

"I'm sorry, what did you just say?" I respond as politely as I can, turning to Dr. Smith, hoping he didn't notice me zoning out.

"I was just wondering if you wanted this," he repeats, holding out a pack of different colored permanent markers. I tilt my head to the side, confused. "For people to sign your cast," he adds, seeing my disoriented expression.

"Oh, um, sure," I reply and he gently sets them down in front of me. I pick them up and hold them tightly in my pale hands. My knuckles turned white from gripping the markers too hard but I don't pay attention. I am trying to be more focused on what the adults are talking about now, not wanting to get in trouble again. Soon though, I am already drifting into a trance, unable to stop myself.

I imagine getting home and seeing Alex running up to hug me, welcoming me back. I see dad standing slightly behind him, waiting to get a turn to check on his little girl. It's such a wonderful scene, the type of moment that always seems to happen at the end of movies to symbolize a happily ever after. In my mind, tangible love fills the air and you can see the people in the room come together as one.

But all of that changes when I am jerked out of my thoughts again. I snap awake to see the long line of never ending walls and lights ahead of me. I immediately know where I am based on the dreary colors and cool temperature. I am back in the same hallway that used to feel so eerie and creepy, except now, it is different.

This time, I noticed the small, rectangular shaped windows that lined the ceiling of the hall, something I had not seen before today. There is wallpaper with every different kind of animal you can imagine, designed to give the little kids that come here something to smile about. I think about how sad I had been the past few days and how awful this corridor had seemed not too long ago. It is like my whole world has changed around me, giving

me a new perspective on life.

My mom soon takes notice of the much more cheerful

grin that I am wearing, compared to my gloomy expression prior

to our conversation with Dr. Smith.

"I knew we would be getting good news soon," she

whispers in my ear, and for once, I actually agree with her. This is

amazing news, and I am the happiest I have been in a long time.

chapter 9:

I go back to my room and start to pack up the one bag my mother had thought to bring for me. I only have a few things here in the hospital, including *Little Women* and some clothes, both clean and dirty. I also have to remember all of the cards, flowers, balloons, and teddy bears that had shown up in my room while I was unconscious, and a few that were more recent.

Soon enough I am ready to leave. My mom picks up all of my stuff and a nurse is poised behind me, ready to spring into action whenever necessary. As we stop in the doorframe, I turn around to look at the room behind me. The messy, unmade bed, the fluorescent lights, the small television up in the top corner of the two walls opposite my bed.

If my life was a movie this would be the moment where I would slowly look back and say, *You know what, I think I'll miss this place.* But my life isn't a movie, and I wasn't going to mourn the death of my life in this hospital room. Not at all. Not even for a second.

"I think I'm ready to go home," I tell my mom, scootching in my seat so that I am facing her.

"Alrighty then, let's go!" she responds. I can tell she is very ecstatic about going back to our house. She wants things to be as close to normal as I do. We both know there are a lot of hardships to come, but for now, I feel great. Free, even. And freedom tastes so sweet.

We navigate the bright halls of the institution with no trouble. We go past all of the individual rooms and then finally through the waiting rooms and out the main doors.

The fresh air feels amazing on my skin. The warmth of the sun, the soft touch of an early autumn breeze on my cheeks, the glare of the natural light in my eyes, even the smell of the city air, cause my body to fill to the brim with joy and comfort. I haven't been outside in days, and I know that doesn't seem like too long, but I'm not meant to be cooped up, I need to be

unrestricted and liberated.

I take a moment to soak in all of the senses around me

but I don't have very long until we arrive at my family's dark blue

Subaru.

As soon as I see the car, flashbacks start to come back to

me. I do my best to hide it and try to cover it up with a smile,

letting my face show a different emotion than my mind, and the

feeling disappears relatively quickly.

I am able to get into the backseat of the car without

much trouble as the nurse helps my mom lift me in. Once sitting

in my usual spot, I rest my head on the headrest and look up

through the skylight on the roof. The bright blue sky and the

shimmering sun shine right into my eyes, but it feels warm, like

the whole world is smiling at me, and for the first time in a while,

it feels like things are going to be okay.

I force my gaze back down towards the driver's seat and see my mom quickly thanking the nurse before she hops into the car and turns around to look at me.

"Comfy?" she asks, raising her eyebrows. I shrug my shoulders and scootch around a bit trying to find a way to comfortably situate my legs in such a small space with their thick casts, but don't end up finding a solution.

"As comfy as I'll ever be I guess," I respond. She sighs and turns to face the windshield, shifting the car into reverse and backing out of the parking spot.

It is nearly silent as we are driving. The radio is softly playing some upbeat song that I don't know but besides that, neither of us starts talking. I focus my attention out the window and watch as all the familiar sights of my home flash by in a blur. I sit still and try to think about normal things, like memories of school or my friends, but everything ends up leading back to the quiet pain in my legs. It has been dulled because of the pain medication they gave me but there is still pressure building up in my lower body, like my feet are about to burst open if I don't get them elevated soon.

The original excitement of being back in the world has faded, and now I just want to get back home, into my own bedroom with my own bed and my own soft pillows and blankets.

We keep driving in silence, passing many monuments of my old life, a park where I used to love to sit and have picnics, some tennis courts, an old ice cream parlor, and a few restaurants where I usually hang out with my friends. All of these places pass by in a blur, and I barely have time to register where we are.

Finally, we turn into my neighborhood, and I know we are close to home. We pass one last sight before I am able to rest, and this one I am able to recognize with full clarity: Natalie's house.

We pass by in what seems like slow motion. I look out at the large white house with its perfect exterior, the flawlessly manicured lawn, the beautiful flower beds, the bright blue door and the wreath of vivid yellow and pink flowers that sits atop it.

The house where, only a few days ago, everything was perfect. Now, even though the outside appears unchanged, I know the inside is broken and damaged. I wonder if Natalie is back at home yet, but before I can look at the house further, we have already passed it and we are back home.

Mom stops the car in the garage and turns back to look at me again, eyes wide and questioning.

"Ready to try this?" she asks.

I smile at her. "As ready as I'll ever be," I respond.

"Okay then let's do this thing!" she says while grinning at me. She gives me one last nod before she opens her door and climbs out of the car.

She heads to the trunk of the car and heaves it open. I try to turn around to look at what she is doing and see her pulling my wheelchair out of the car and unfolding it. She closes the trunk and pushes the chair around to my side of the car. She opens the door and puts the brakes on the chair, making sure it stays in place. She puts one arm behind my back and the other under my knees and picks me up like a baby. I am soon placed gently into

my wheelchair and my mom locks the car and wheels me into our

house.

I greet my dad and brother but tell them I am too tired to

do anything. Everyone agrees to let me sleep and Dad carries me

to my room and places me in my bed. He and my mom tuck me

in like they used to when I was a little kid and they leave me alone

to rest. As soon as they close the door, I fall into a deep,

dreamless, sleep.

chapter 10:

"Are you positive she should be going back to school so soon?"

"Oh, come on Katherine, we both know she's ready, she's been home for five weeks already, she needs to get back to her schoolwork. She's falling too far behind and I know deep down, you agree with me."

"I'm just not so sure that it's the right time, that's all."

"It will never be the right time, we've just got to do it. She's been practicing and she's practically a pro in that wheelchair, she's not on strong pain medication anymore, and she wants to see her friends. She needs to connect with people again."

"I know but Jack-"

"You both know I'm sitting right here don't you? Stop talking about me like I'm not here," I butt in. Both of my parents look at me as though they have completely forgotten that they had invited me to join in on this conversation.

"Well, what do you think then?" my mom questions

kindly.

"I definitely want to go back to school." She starts to

object but I stop her before she can get a word in. "Come on, I'll

be fine, my friends will help me, all of my teachers know what's

going on and so does the nurse, Ms. Robinson. Nothing bad is

going to happen. I want to be able to enjoy my junior year as

much as I can."

My parents both turn to look at each other again and I

see my mother give a small nod to my dad.

"You'll start on Monday then!" my dad exclaims. I grin

excitedly and he leans down to hug me. I've never been so happy

to be going to school in my entire life. I am so delighted that I do

a little spin in my chair and both of my parents laugh, clearly

happy that I am happy.

The last few weeks at home have been pretty hard. I've

had to learn how to live my life in a whole new way. But by now,

I'm used to it, and I'm finally starting to adjust to the new normal.

Natalie was able to go back to school right away and she's been over to see me a few times. She usually brings me my school work so that I don't fall too far behind everybody else, but I'm still not completely caught up yet. I've also had countless appointments at the hospital with Dr. Smith. I'm ashamed to say, he's starting to grow on me. He's pretty nice to me and I can tell he is trying his best to try to make things easier on me. Between all of those appointments and my schoolwork, I've been very busy.

I've been begging my parents for the past week to let me go back to school, and they finally agreed to talk about it tonight. I am so happy that I will be going back in just two days! I guess I am a little nervous about how things will be once I go back, with no Daisy to keep me company in science class or walking down the hallways with me.

Daisy's parents had her funeral while I was still in the hospital, so I wasn't able to attend, but I've been to her headstone since then. It was so odd, to see someone's whole life reduced to just one cold piece of rock. It was sad, but it also brought me a sense of closure, a realization that everything had been real.

I hear my mom clear her throat, startling me from my thoughts and bringing me back to the present.

I look up at her, "Sorry, what?" I ask, clearly I missed something while I was thinking to myself.

"I was just asking if you need any new school supplies before you go back?" she explains.

I think for a second, ticking off each item I should need. I remember Natalie buying me everything I was supposed to get for this year a few weeks ago so I'm hoping I'm good.

"No, I think I should be fine," I respond. She nods and turns to leave the room.

"I think I'll just go to bed then, if that's alright with you two?" Mom looks back towards Dad and we both nod at her. She gives me a warm smile and walks over to hug me again. After our embrace, she swirls towards the hallway and joyfully strolls upstairs to bed.

Dad and I stay silent as we hear her footsteps recede up the staircase. Finally he breaks the silence.

"Well I would say that went well! Wouldn't you?" While he asks this, he turns abruptly towards me and I look up at him. He is grinning from ear to ear.

"I would say so, yes!" I reply and we both chuckle. I meet his smiling eyes and beam back at him.

We stay in the kitchen talking for a few minutes before we both agree we should be going to bed too.

I abruptly open my eyes, squinting at the bright rays of sunlight that are shining through the thin curtains into my room. The screeching of my alarm clock, something I usually hate, makes me feel a burst of happiness. It is finally Monday! I never in a million years thought I would be so relieved to be waking up at six in the morning to go to school. I am so insanely excited to be getting back to normal!

Just as I switch off the alarm, someone knocks on my door but before I can even answer, my mom bustles in.

She runs to the other side of my room and opens my closet door, picking up the outfit I had set aside last night.

"Good morning sweetie! Are you excited for your first day back at school?" She brings the clothes over to my bed as I enthusiastically nod to answer her question. I sit up and she helps me take my pajamas off and together we pull my new clothes on. I am wearing one of my favorite shirts, a white one with little yellow sunflowers scattered all over it, with the same baggy jean shorts I have to wear almost every day, considering they are one of my only pairs that fit over the large casts on my feet.

We are able to continue the rest of my morning routine without much trouble. I brush my teeth, comb my hair, and eat the same breakfast that I ate every morning before school prior to the accident, two scrambled eggs and a slice of toast. Everything feels normal and I love it.

Just as I am finishing up at the kitchen table, Alex comes skidding downstairs to eat his breakfast. He just started sixth grade and he begins a half hour later than I do now. I watch him run into the mud room to grab his backpack and then he comes back and starts making his lunch, ignoring both myself and Mom, who is standing at the kitchen island right behind me. She raises her eyebrows at me and I grin and shrug in response. That boy can never sit still.

"Well good morning to you too Alex," Mom chuckles as she walks around the island to stand behind him and ruffle his hair.

"Oh, sorry! Good morning Mommy!" he says hurriedly while going up on his tiptoes to kiss her cheek. He then quickly turns back to packing the sloppy sandwich that he just made and a bag of chips into his lunch box.

He starts to zip it up, but before he can get very far Mom stops him, "Hey Al?"

"Yeah, Mommy?"

"Aren't you forgetting something?"

"Ummm, nope, I don't think so!" he replies, and tries to run around her, clearly trying to hide something. Alex is a terrible liar.

"Are you sure?" my mom questions, a playful twinkle in her eyes. She grabs an apple from the blue fruit bowl in the middle of the island and waves it in the air.

Alex's nose scrunches up and I can tell he is about to give in. "Mom please don't make me take fruit with me! I hate it! Jackson's mom doesn't make him eat ANY fruits or vegetables!"

Mom and I both laugh loudly and she tosses him the apple. He reluctantly catches it and shoves it into his lunch box.

"Are you ready to get going Abigail?" my mom asks me as she swings my backpack over one shoulder and jabs her thumb towards the garage door.

"I think so!" I wheel myself out from my position at the table and push myself towards the garage. "Have a great day at school Al! I'll see you later!" I yell back over my shoulder.

"Thanks! You too Abby!" he replies.

Mom opens the door but then calls back into the kitchen, "I'll be right back to drive you to school after I drop off Abby, okay Alex? Be ready by seven forty please!"

"Yeah, alright," he responds, with a slightly cooler tone than he used with me.

We climb into the car and my mom folds up my wheelchair and puts it in the trunk. Soon, we're on the road and I watch the familiar buildings pass by as we drive the well known route to school, for the first time in forever.

chapter 11:

Our car slowly rolls into the parking lot of Stonebrook

High School. As we pull into a parking spot, I look out the

window and see all of the students walking around, talking to

their friends, getting ready to go to class. My peers, who I have

known almost my entire life, seem so different than they did a few

months ago. I guess I just have a different perspective on things.

Throughout my school career I have been at the top of the social

food chain, but now, I fear I have slipped down a few notches. I

wonder what people will think of me now that I'm in a

wheelchair and can't walk?

My mom turns to me and I give her an uneasy half-smile.

She seems to read my mind.

"Don't worry honey, I'm sure everything is going to go

great, you'll have your friends and teachers to support you

whenever you need help and I'm sure all of the kids will be happy

that you are back. I give her a little nod and take a deep breath.

Mom leaves the car to pull out my chair and I sit in the front seat, waiting for her to come around to my door.

When we finally get the whole wheelchair thing situated, Mom walks with me into the school. I have to go to the nurse's office before class to get my elevator pass, and Mom has to come with me.

As I push myself through the school hallways, I feel strangely uneasy, like I don't belong here. The version of me that was last here at this school seems so far gone, I feel like I'm a different person. My mom and I don't talk the whole way to Ms. Robinson's office. We pass quite a few students in the hallways, on their way to their first periods. I try to smile at the ones I know, but most of them avoid my gaze, look uncomfortable, and look at me with pity.

We soon get everything sorted with the nurse and it is time for me to finally go to class. My mom kisses me on the cheek and whispers a *good luck* in my ear before she walks back out the double doors into the parking lot. Ms. Robinson offers to walk me to my first class, but I tell her I know my way around and I remember what the classroom looks like from the first day, so I should be fine.

She lets me leave and I wheel out of her office, heading towards the stairwell that I usually take, before I remember I can't exactly use the stairs anymore.

I ride the elevator up to the second floor where I have calculus for my earliest class of the day. There is a quiet *ding* and the doors open into the long hallway that seems to stretch on for miles and miles. Both sides of the corridor are filled with hundreds of navy blue lockers.

Room 211, that is where I am supposed to be. I am looking down both ways of the hall when something about twenty lockers to the left of me catches my eye.

I start down the hallway, towards the deep blue locker that caught my gaze. I know before I even get there, that this is Daisy's locker.

Students decorated the locker so that it had turned into a memorial for Daisy. There were hundreds of flowers piled below the locker and taped onto the door. Someone had placed and lit five large candles surrounding the flowers on the ground, and a large picture of Daisy is hanging in the middle of the door. In the photo, Daisy is smiling, bright as ever into the camera with her curly red hair flowing effortlessly around her face.

My eyes begin to burn and tears start to stream quietly down my face.

"I'm so sorry Daisy," I whisper, so quietly that even I can barely hear myself. The tears continue to fall into my lap as I stare at the memorial. I look down at the flowers on the ground. No surprise, most of them were daisies.

Suddenly a memory from years ago flashes back through my head, a memory I had forgotten about until now.

We were on a school camping trip in eighth grade. We had to spend the night outside, sleeping in sleeping bags but neither Daisy nor I could sleep.

84

Soon enough, the sky had started to lighten and we tried to sneak out of the

campsite, to a field that we had seen earlier nearby. We wanted to watch the

sunrise by ourselves.

"Shhhhh Daisy you have to be quiet!" I whisper and we both can't

help but to giggle.

"Oh relax, Abby, no one's going to catch us!"

"You don't know that." I accused.

"Yes I do!" she insisted.

"How?"

"Because I'm a genius! And geniuses don't get caught!" More giggles

from both of us.

We crept along in the near darkness until we reached the trail we

had hiked up earlier. Daisy led the way. We walked for about five minutes

downhill before we saw a small clearing in the trees and turned off the path,

only to see a wide open field of tall grass and wildflowers. The field sat on top

of a hill, and in front of us, I could see the sun starting to shine above the

horizon.

We walked to the middle of the meadow and sat down in the flowers. Neither of us talked, we just sat there in awe as the sun climbed above the mountains in the distance and we could feel the warmth on our faces.

"That was the most beautiful thing I have ever seen," muttered Daisy. I hummed in response, still fascinated by the sight ahead of me.

After a while we tore ourselves away and got up to go back to the camp. Before we left, I picked up one of the flowers from the ground.

"Hey Daisy! Look, it's a daisy, just like your name!"

She gave me a sort of sour look.

"What's wrong, you don't like daisies?" I asked.

"Not really, no. I'm sorry, I know I'm supposed to, because of my name and all but I just..."

"It's fine, it's alright. I don't care if you don't like daisies," I quickly said and the big smile returned to her face. "In fact, I don't like them either!" I yelled, throwing the daisy to the ground. We laughed for a few moments before Daisy spoke again.

"I've never told anybody that," she noted.

"Well, I'm glad you told me," I replied.

Daisy and I looked at each other and laughed the entire way back to our sleeping bags.

Tears continue to stream down my face in the present, standing in front of Daisy's locker. Even though I am still crying, I chuckle as I see all of the daisies. I guess I really was the only one she ever told. I make a mental note to go buy her flowers tomorrow before school so that I can add to the memorial.

I clean up my face and then wheel towards room 211. I am ready to get back to reality.

As I reach the entrance to the classroom, I take a deep breath and reach for the door handle, before I realize I can't open the door like that anymore, I have to use the handicap button on the side. I inhale and exhale deeply to ready myself again and then push the button. The door glides open easily and I wheel myself into the classroom.

Immediately, everyone is staring right at me. The teacher must have been in the middle of a lesson, as the whole class is silent and he is standing at the front of the room.

"Welcome! Abigail, right?" the teacher greets me. I nod silently and the teacher sticks out his right hand and gives me a warm smile. I quickly shake it.

"My name is Mr. Carson, I will be your math teacher for this year. Do you remember me from your first day of school?"

I shrug, still silent. I hate everyone staring at me like this.

"Okay! Well anyway, that's your desk at the front right there, you can take a seat and we'll get started!" I mutter a quiet thank you and wheel to the empty spot in the front right corner of the room. There is no seat so I can just stay in my wheelchair.

It's not until I have taken out my notebook and pencil and Mr. Carson starts talking again that I actually look around and see who I am sitting next to.

I am immediately startled by how familiar he looks. I don't know him and I am sure I have only seen this boy a few times in school, but still, his features are so recognizable to me, as if I have seen them a hundred times.

While Mr. Carson drones on, I look over at his paper to see the name at the top.

Elias Smith. Dr. Smith. That's why he is so familiar! I've seen his face a million times on Dr. Smith's desk! He was a lot younger, sure, but his features have remained the same. He looks even more similar to his dad now than he did then, with his bright green eyes and messy light brown hair.

He quickly turns his head around to look at me. I swirl my head back to look at the blank piece of paper in front of me, my cheeks flushing bright pink. I must have been staring at him too long and I think he definitely noticed.

I try to focus on the lesson but I can't stop thinking about what a coincidence this is. I mean, he's Dr. Smith's son! I wonder if he knows who I am?

Soon enough Mr. Carson tells us we can start to pack up our stuff since there are only five minutes left of class.

Immediately everyone starts talking and getting up to find their

friends. I don't know anybody in this class though, and even if I

did, I couldn't get through the huge crowd of students to find

them. As I am trying to grab my backpack from the back of my

chair, a voice speaks from next to me.

"Hey there! Your name is Abigail right?"

I whip around and see Elias beaming at me, he's still in

his seat too, I guess he doesn't know anybody either.

I smile back at him and say, "I am, and what's your

name?" Of course I know the answer to that question but I'm not

letting him know that.

"I'm Elias." He responds. "Elias Smith." He's still

grinning at me.

"Oh! You don't happen to be related to a Dr. Andrew

Smith do you? He's my doctor at the Children's Hospital," I ask,

as though I have not already figured that out. I need to be sure,

there are a lot of Smiths in this school, let alone in the entire city.

"I actually am, yeah, that's my dad! Hopefully you don't hold that against me," he jokes.

I laugh. "Of course not, I love your dad! He's been an amazing help to me since the accident."

"That's cool!" There are a few moments of silence where neither of us has anything to say but then it is broken.

The loud sound of the bell ringing drowns out all of the talking and everybody rushes towards the doors.

"Well, it was nice talking to you, I guess I'll see you tomorrow," Elias tells me. I wave at him and he walks out of the classroom.

This time, navigating the hallways is slightly harder as there are hundreds of students flooding them. But, even with so many familiar faces, no one seems to want to talk to me or even say hello. I even see Natalie in the hallway, but she barely looks at me. It is as though no one thinks of me as a real person anymore. They don't see me as me.

By the time lunch comes around, I'm already exhausted. Keeping up my normal school schedule is proving harder than I ever thought it would be. I get myself out the courtyard pretty easily since there are no steps or ledges I have to navigate. I am just starting to turn my head around, trying to find the people I used to eat with when I get a text from Natalie.

Natalie : Hey! Forgot to tell you, Jake is driving us to the nearest fast food restaurant for lunch so we aren't there. Want anything?

Of course they left, not a single one of them has even said a word to me today. Even Natalie has been especially rude to me now that I'm back at school. It's almost like she's avoiding me. I hope that she's just having an off day and that's not the case. I respond to the text.

Abigail : I'm good, I have food. Talk when you get back?

She reads the message but doesn't respond. I try to stop thinking about Natalie and look around for someone I know. There's no one that I am good friends with, and to make matters worse, everyone in the courtyard is avoiding my gaze, as if they don't want me to notice them.

I end up finding myself a nice, shady corner to sit in and park my chair there. I grab my backpack and unhook it from the back of my wheelchair, setting it on a bench right next to me. I reach into my bag and pull out the lunchbox my mom had packed for me earlier this morning. This day isn't turning out quite the way I had hoped it would.

Tears start to grow in the corners of my eyes as I think about the events of today. I unwrap my sandwich from it's tinfoil and sit quietly until that silence is interrupted.

"Hey! Abigail!" I look up to find out who is calling my name and see Elias jogging towards me with a goofy smile on his face. I wipe the tears from my eyes and grin back at him. I don't want him to know I have been crying. He quickly makes it over to where I am eating and sits down on the bench, right next to my backpack.

He turns to me, his mouth open and ready to speak, but stops abruptly when he sees my face.

"Hey, are you okay? What's wrong?" he asks me. So he does know that I was crying.

I am about to immediately go to the default answer of "nothing" but he looks so concerned, with his brows furrowed and that huge smile turned into a frown. I would feel bad if I didn't just tell him the truth.

I hesitate for a moment but eventually say, "It's just that I feel like everyone is avoiding me today, including my so-called friends. No one has said a word to me since I got back…"

He raises his eyebrows and I laugh, "except for you of course!" He nods in approval.

"But everyone else here has been dodging me all day. In fact, my best friend is at some fast food place right now with all of my other friends getting lunch without me because I wasn't invited. They left before I even had the chance to go with them."

"Well that explains why you were sitting here all by yourself looking so miserable," he jokes.

I scoff "I am not miserable!"

"I didn't say you ARE miserable, I said you WERE miserable. Past tense. Everything's better now that I'm here." Elias points his thumbs in at his chest in a big, silly, gesture, causing me to burst out in laughter.

"Ha! You wish!" We are both laughing now.

Once the giggling subsides, we both start to eat our lunches. We talk about everyday things, our morning classes, homework we have so far, what we're doing after school today. He asks about my legs and the crash and I give him as many details as I can remember.

Soon though, the bell rings and it's time to go back to class and face the rest of the students again.

"Do you think you could give me your phone number?" I request before we head inside. He raises his eyebrows at me and I panic. I come up with the quickest excuse I can think of. "You know, so that if I ever need to contact your dad when he's not at work I can just text you or something?"

He chuckles, "You know I was going to give you my number before the whole flustered explanation you just gave." I blush furiously and look down at my lap.

"Here, give me your phone," he suggests. I hand him mine and he hands me his. We both put our contacts in the other's phones and hand them back to each other.

Elias stands up and holds his hand out to me. I reach my arm out to reach his and he shakes my hand enthusiastically.

"It was a pleasure eating lunch with you Miss!" he declares.

I giggle and respond, "Thank you, good sir, I hope to eat with you again in the near future!"

"I look forward to it!" he exclaims. He tips an imaginary hat to me and spins on his heel, towards the doors inside.

While he walks back inside, I put my backpack onto my lap and start towards my own classroom, in the opposite direction of Elias'. I stop just before the threshold of the door. *Here we go again.* And I push myself through.

chapter 12:

The rest of the day goes by in a blur. In all of my afternoon classes I get the same reactions that I did all morning. No one looks at, talks to, or even recognizes me unless they are forced to. I don't have any of my later classes with Natalie or any of my old friends. I am supposed to have my seventh period science class with Elias, but he texts me the period before to tell me that he has a dentist appointment and isn't going to be there. So, I didn't really talk to anyone until my mom comes to pick me up.

I find my mom's car relatively easily, she always parks in the same area when she picks me up from school. When she spots me wheeling towards the car, she gets out of the driver's seat and comes to help me with my wheelchair. As soon as we are both in the car and exiting the parking lot, the interrogation starts.

She speaks very quickly, firing one question after another, never even stopping for air. "How was your day honey? What was it like? Did you have fun? Were your friends glad to have you

back? Was anyone mean to you? You know you can tell me if

anyone was mean to you and I'll make sure they never hurt you

again baby -"

"Whoa, Mom! Slow down, okay? My day was okay"

But before I can even finish, she interjects again, clearly

worried about me. "Just okay? What happened? Are you alright?"

"Mom! I'm fine! It was just a little hard getting back into

the routine of things, that's all."

She seems to accept that answer. "Okay, okay that's good

then. How was it, seeing all your old friends again?"

I don't know what to tell her. I certainly don't want her to

worry about Natalie for me, I mean, for all I know, Natalie was

just having an off day and not seeing her was just a coincidence. I

decide to tell her, but make sure she knows it's no big deal.

"I didn't really see anyone, including Natalie-" I say

calmly.

99

"Well, why is that?" She's getting defensive again, I can see it in her eyes.

"We just don't have any classes together and she already had plans to go off campus for lunch today so I didn't really get the chance to talk to her," I replied.

She nods quietly. I can tell she's not happy with Natalie so I tell her more about my day.

"I did meet a new friend though!"

Her face lights up. "Really?! That's great! Who is it?"

"Actually he's Dr. Smith's son, Elias. I'm sure you've heard of him," I answer, smiling.

"Oh! That's great, sweetie! Is he nice?"

"Yeah! I talked to him in math class and he sat next to me at lunch so I wasn't all alone when Natalie left." I revealed.

"That's amazing! So overall your day was good?"

"I guess so, yeah," I conclude.

We continue through the streets towards home when all of a sudden, we make a wrong turn.

"Wait! Mom, where are you going? Home is back there!"
I question.

"What do you mean? Oh, Abby did you forget?"

"Forget what?"

"We have an appointment with Dr. Smith today!" I'm still
confused, I didn't remember an appointment.

"You seriously forgot? Abby, you're getting your casts off
today? How do you not remember that?" she wonders,
incredulous.

I gasp. Oh my gosh! She's right I am getting them off
today! I must have forgotten amidst all the excitement of school!

"Oh shoot, I totally blanked! Yes, I can't wait!" I do a
little happy dance in my seat and my mom laughs. I can't believe
that the appointment is today! I can finally get my casts off, which
means I can wear normal shoes again, and pants that aren't super
baggy!

I keep doing my little happy dance until we get to Dr.
Smith's office.

Dr. Smith enters the room and immediately moves towards his computer, opening the x-rays that were taken of my legs a few moments ago. After the images are pulled up, Dr. Smith looks at me with a grin on his face. It reminds me of Elias beaming at me earlier.

"So, Abigail, I have some good news for you!" he announces.

I smile back at him and he continues, "Your x-rays look amazing! Your legs are healing extraordinarily well, much better than even I had expected, and I think that, in time, and with a lot of practice, you may be able to walk again!"

My jaw drops to the floor. I am shocked to my core. I can't believe it! I thought I would never be out of this wheelchair, never get to be normal again, never get to drive, or go up stairs, or play my favorite sports for the rest of my life. My whole body is filled with butterflies, my heart is pounding in my ears. I am ecstatic!

"But, you said-" I stammer.

"I know what I said, and I was wrong, you are going to be able to walk again, Abigail!"

My spirits are lifted, everything is going to be okay. I will be okay.

My mom looks just as happy as I do, but of course, she's the first one to speak to ask Dr. Smith about the specifics of my ability to walk. While they talk, I just sit and listen.

He explains how I will have to go through extensive physical therapy at least three times a week, and in time I will be able to walk with crutches, and then, eventually, on my own. He says that the process will likely take five to six months until I am fully mobile again, but I don't care. At least there is an end in sight now.

The rest of the visit goes by in a blur. The casts are taken off of my legs and soon it is time to go home.

I feel so free on the car ride home. In just a few short months, I will be able to return to my regular routine. I am full of pure joy.

That night, we order Indian food from my favorite restaurant and have a celebratory dinner. When we tell my dad and Alex the news, both of them react the same way as Mom and I. Everyone in the house is so cheerful, it feels as though everything in the world is perfect. The four of us sit and talk for a while and then we watch TV together until it is time for bed.

That night, after I am tucked and cozy under my fuzzy blanket, I think about the events of the day. And the strange part is, although I was upset earlier about Natalie and everybody, I don't really think I care. I realize that I had a good day, regardless, and that is all due to members of the Smith family.

chapter 13:

The next day I wake up feeling, well, firstly, very tired, but overall pretty good. I use my arms to push myself up into a sitting position and soon my mom barges into the room. We exchange good mornings as she grabs my clothes for me and helps me get ready for the day.

Once I am all set, my dad carries me downstairs and I wheel myself to the kitchen table where my breakfast is already waiting. My mom stands at the island making a peanut butter and jelly sandwich and gathering the rest of the food for my lunch. Alex isn't downstairs yet so it is pretty quiet and still. I take a big bite of my toast and a swig of water before I start up a conversation. While I'm thinking of what to say, I remember a thought that was lost in the chaos of yesterday afternoon, Daisy's locker.

"Hey, Mom?" I ask.

She looks up from my lunch to meet my eyes. "Yeah, Abby? What's up?" She sounds a little bit concerned, like she fears I am hurt.

"Do you think we could leave for school a little bit early today? Some kids at school have put flowers and candles by Daisy's locker and I wanted to contribute something," I share.

She gives me a warm grin. "Of course, honey! That sounds like a great idea," she approves. I smile back at her and continue eating.

A few minutes later, Alex comes bounding down the stairs so recklessly, I don't know how he doesn't fall on his face. As soon as he is in the room, the peacefulness of a few minutes ago fades away.

Alex goes about his usual morning routine but talks the entire time. I don't catch much of what he is saying because he's speaking so fast, firing off word after word. He moves through the space like a tornado, going so quickly that no one else has a chance to get a word in. Mom opens her mouth a few times but never actually gets the chance to speak.

I keep watching them as Alex continues rambling on. My mom makes eye contact with me and rolls her eyes playfully. We both chuckle but Alex is still in his own little world. I think he is talking about some video game he wants to get, or maybe it's just an app for his phone? Like I said, it's hard to tell. Our mom is now nodding along and humming every so often but I don't think she is really listening.

I sit silently and eat until all of my food is gone. I look at the clock on the microwave. It's only six forty five but if we want to pick up some flowers before school, we have to leave now. My brother is still ranting with no signs of stopping so I get my mom's attention and tap my wrist where a watch would sit if I was wearing one.

She seems to get the hint and shuts my lunchbox, pushes it into my backpack, and we both start heading towards the door.

After a few steps we hear Alex calling out from behind us. Apparently he finally snapped out of his debate with himself.

"Wait, Mommy! Abby! Where are you guys going?" he objects.

"I've got to take Abigail to school Al!" my mom laughs.

He quickly glances at the clock. "Already?"

Mom walks over and plants a kiss on the top of his head. "We have to make a stop on the way, but I'll still be back in time to pick you up, okay?" He nods and she ruffles his hair and then makes her way back to me.

Before we cross through the doorway into the garage, I wave goodbye to Alex and tell him to have a good day.

The grocery store is on the way to school and is only a few minutes away from our house, so we get there very quickly. It's not very crowded considering it's still so early in the morning so we are able to park right next to the doors.

We decide that since we only need one thing, Mom will run in and I will stay in the car. Before she leaves, she asks me

what kind of flowers I want to get. I tell her anything but daisies.
She tilts her head a little to the right and gives me a puzzled look
but doesn't say anything. She just bobs her head and climbs out
of the car.

I lock the doors behind her and stay in the car, waiting for
her to come back.

While I am sitting there, I scroll through the social media
apps on my phone. I end up looking at my profile. I don't have
any new posts from the last couple of weeks. I didn't feel the need
to document my injuries for my whole school to see, so I haven't
written anything or posted any pictures since before the accident.
I used to be so active online. Every meal I ate, every activity I did,
every selfie I took, went up on my feed.

I hit an icon on the bottom of the screen and go back to
the home page. Natalie is still very active on social media. Even
though it's barely past seven in the morning, as I scroll down, I
can already count three posts of hers, just from today.

I keep mindlessly scrolling for a few more minutes until, all of a sudden, there is a sharp tap on the driver's side window. I jump and my head jerks up, scanning for danger.

Fortunately it's only Mom. She gives me a small wave and I unlock the doors so that she can climb back in.

Once she is settled in her seat, she hands me a beautiful bouquet of bright red roses. She stares at me sympathetically, waiting for a response. I give her a look that I hope is warm and comforting.

"They're perfect, Mom. Thank you," I whispered.

She brushes a stray strand of hair out of my eyes and cups her right hand around my cheek. Her hand feels so soft and warm on my face and I let my eyelids fall for a moment, taking everything in. When I open my eyes, she gives me a familiar smile and answers, "Of course, honey, anything I can do to help."

We drive in silence the rest of the way to school, but it's a comfortable silence. Like we have a mutual understanding that neither of us really has anything to say.

After what seems like no time at all, we slowly roll into the school parking lot. This time, because Mom doesn't have to come in with me, we keep driving all the way up to the front of the drop off line, right by the entrance.

We take a little longer than some of the other students, as I need help getting out of the car, but I don't think anyone really minds.

Mom helps me get everything situated quickly and, with a rapid exchange of "have a good day" and "love you!" I am on my way inside.

As I wheel through the hallways, I have the roses in my lap. I am going to need them soon anyway so I figure it will be easier not to go through the trouble of putting them in and taking them out of my bag. I remember the way to Daisy's locker from yesterday, so I'm able to get there without any mistakes.

The corridors are relatively crowded with lots of kids, but people move out of the way for me and there is a sort of bubble around her locker, where no one is walking.

I roll myself into that bubble and just sit there for a minute. People are around me in every direction, but no one is paying any attention to me anyway, so I tune them out.

I look at the pile of scattered daisies all around the floor and taped to the actual door of the locker. There is not one single flower there that is not a daisy. I mean, I can imagine why. I'm sure every person who put one down thought they were being clever.

Well her name was Daisy, so daisies are the perfect flowers to place in her memory, right?

And I'm the only one who knows that's wrong. I set the bouquet of roses on the ground, right in the middle of the memorial, so that they are easy to see.

I'm sure people will wonder who put them here, probably thinking that it was someone who didn't know her. Someone who didn't even know her name, but wanted to pay their respects.

But whenever I go past here, I'll know. I'll know that my case is the exact opposite. I am the *only* one who knew Daisy well

112

enough. Knew her well enough to know that she didn't like daisies.

I leave the flowers there, and turn around to head to math class. *Gosh, math class.* Seems like far too normal of an event to be going to right now, but I don't really have a choice, do I?

It's just so weird to me sometimes, that such a life changing event can happen to me, and yet, I still have to go through my normal routine every day.

Things like school and homework seem so tedious now, so minuscule compared to everything else going on in my life.

At least I'll get to see Elias again.

chapter 14:

The rest of the week goes by fairly quickly. Everyday has been similar to the first two, with most students ignoring me and my old friends avoiding any contact with me. I have seen Natalie a few times, and every time she either whispers something to the person she's with or will just give me an icy cold glare. I know when she whispers she's talking about me but I really couldn't care less at the moment. I have bigger things to worry about.

Elias starts to fill the gap left by Natalie. He and I talk during classes and he still comes to sit with me everyday at lunch. I really enjoy hanging out with him so I'm glad he hasn't gotten sick of me yet. He makes me laugh with his goofy jokes and always seems to cheer me up, no matter what kind of day I'm having.

School is a lot better now that I'm getting into the groove of things again. I've pretty much caught up on the few assignments I still hadn't done and I'm used to my busy schedule again.

Over the weekend, I mostly slept. I was exhausted from my first week back. When I wasn't in bed, my mom and I went shopping for some new clothes for this year, considering we hadn't gotten the chance to in August. Alex, Mom, Dad and I went out to dinner a couple of times at our favorite restaurants. We talked about school and sports and not once did we even have to mention the accident. I was so glad things were going back to the way they used to be.

This morning though, I have to wake up early to my blaring alarm and go back to the reality of doctor appointments and school.

I grudgingly manage to pull myself out of bed, brush my teeth, and get ready for a Monday.

My dad carries me downstairs and I meet my mom for breakfast. When I roll into the kitchen, I am quickly cheered up by the bright rays of sun flooding into the area, and the warm yellow paint on the walls welcoming me. My mom is holding a plate of scrambled eggs in her right hand while she grabs a single slice of toast with her left.

"Good morning!" I say cheerfully. Mom must have not heard me come in, as when I speak, she jumps and almost drops the food she is carrying.

"Oh! Abby! Gosh, you scared me!" she exclaims.

I giggle at her and push myself over to my spot at the kitchen table. She places my plate of food in front of me and I begin to eat.

I can hear the morning news droning on from the television across the room. Our kitchen is completely open to our family room, so I can see the TV from where I am currently sitting. Over the back of the couch, I can see our local news anchors at their desks, talking about everything that's going on today. There's nothing interesting so far today. After all, it's still pretty early.

My mom is back in the kitchen, this time emptying the dishwasher that must've been running after I had gone to bed last night.

At the commercial break, Mom is done with the dishes so she comes and sits across from me.

"So, Abby, are you ready for your physical therapy appointment today?" she questions, raising her eyebrows. Clearly she is excited. I forgot my first session is today! I have been really looking forward to starting physical therapy, but I guess I was so tired that it completely slipped my mind.

I grin and do a little dance in my seat. "Oh my gosh yes! I am *so* excited!" I exclaim.

She laughs and continues talking, "I just got the confirmation text, you're sure you want to go right?"

I scoff jokingly, feigning shock. "Am I sure? Of course I'm sure! I can't wait to walk again!"

"I'm sure you are but you know it'll be a while, right?"

I calm down slightly. "Yeah, I know. I'm just hopeful for the future." I beam at her.

"Good! I just don't want you to be disappointed if things go a little sideways today," she warns.

"I promise you, I won't be disappointed," I reply.

"Great! We'll go straight after school then!" she concludes.

"Awesome!" I agree.

I finish up my breakfast while listening to the TV still playing in the background, and wheel over to put my plate in the sink. My mom gets up too, and grabs my backpack.

"Okay Alex, Abby and I are leaving for school! I'll be back soon for you!" she calls over to the living room. I look over just in time to see a little head pop up above the back of the couch, and I jump.

"Alex!" I startle. "Have you been there this entire time?" I chuckle.

"Yeah?" he says, although it's more of a question. "Wait, did you not notice me?" He begins to laugh too.

"Apparently not!" I admitted.

"You didn't know he was there?" Mom wondered. "Why did you think the TV was playing?"

"I don't know? I thought that you just wanted something on while you were cooking!"

All three of us are shaking with laughter now. After a few seconds, we quiet down and I wave goodbye to Alex.

The rest of the drive to school and getting to class goes by in a blur. I'm used to the usual drive to school now. It's nothing eventful anymore.

We left a little bit later today so I'm one of the last ones to reach my math class. Although, the bell hasn't rung yet so students are still sitting in groups, chatting. I scoot over to my seat at the front of the classroom, next to Elias.

He is already at our desk, silently scrolling through his phone. He has his headphones in, so I tap on his shoulder to get his attention.

He jerks his head up to look at me, obviously startled by my presence, but as soon as he sees that it's just me, I see his eyes immediately relax.

He pulls his earbuds out of his ears and unplugs them from his phone.

I nod at him. "Good morning Elias!"

"Hey Abby!" he greets me, while folding up the cord to put into his backpack. "How're you doing today?"

I start unloading my notebook and pens onto the table. "I'm actually doing pretty well today!" I smile.

"That's great!" he beams.

We keep talking for a few minutes before class starts. We just chat about the usual things, the weather, our classes, homework assignments, etcetera.

Before we know it, Mr. Carson is up at the front of the room and is beginning today's lesson. He drones on about derivatives for the entire period. All we do is sit and take notes and answer a few practice problems. It is very boring today. It seems to last an eternity, but eventually, the bell rings, signaling the end of class.

I say a quick goodbye to Elias before pushing myself to my next period. I don't even have to think about where to go anymore. I've memorized my route and now I can get around easily.

In the next three classes before lunch, nothing exciting happens. I barely pay any attention, because I'm too busy being excited for the end of the day. Whenever I think about my physical therapy appointment after school, I get butterflies in my stomach.

Before I know it, it's already time for lunch. On my way to the courtyard to meet Elias, I spot Natalie talking to a few other girls, who I used to be friends with, standing right by her locker. These days I don't usually give her a second look, but I'm in such a good mood today, I decide to give it a try.

I wheel over to them, but Natalie's back is to me so she doesn't seem to notice. Once I reach the group, I lightly tap on Natalie's back and she whips around to face me. At first she is looking for someone up higher, above my head. But then, slowly, her eyes move down to meet mine.

She meets my gaze and smirks at me. I already know that this is a mistake.

chapter 15:

"What do you want, Abigail?" she sneers, rolling her eyes.

I instantly feel belittled, like I am no more than a little kid. I decide to brush it off, and try to be nice to her; maybe she's just in a bad mood today, but then again, I seem to be using that excuse for her a lot lately.

"Well?" she scoffs. "Are you going to talk or what?"

I build up some courage. "Um… I was just going to ask you something, but it can wait if you're um… if you're… you're busy right now?" It comes out like a question, even though I didn't mean it to. I've never felt so intimidated, especially not in front of my so-called best friend.

"Just spit it out, I don't have time for this," she snaps.

I am slightly taken aback by her attitude, but I continue.

"I was just… um… just wondering or… asking… or…"

"ABIGAIL!" They were all staring at me now.

"Okay, okay. I have my first physical therapy appointment this afternoon and I was wondering if you would maybe want to come with me? You know? And we could hang out like we used to?" As soon as I'm done talking, I regret it immediately. She starts to laugh, but not in a pleasant way. The other girls join in, and it feels like a slap in the face.

The wicked witch speaks, "Oh! Abigail, you don't really think that we still want to be friends with you, do you?" she mocks.

"I don't - I just - I guess I just thought -" I stammer.

"Thought what? That we would want to be seen with someone like you? No way! Can you imagine?" she jeers. She starts to laugh again, and her minions join in. "Sorry Abby, but you don't fit in my life anymore."

I feel so humiliated and so dumb. She's right, why would she want to be friends with me? I'm useless. Heck, even I wouldn't want to hang out with me.

I'm just about to turn away, when I hear someone calling my name from down the hall.

"Abigail?" I look up, fresh tears in my eyes, and see none other than Elias, jogging towards us. He looks concerned, so I think he must have seen me crying. Once he reaches me I give him a weak smile, but he looks furious. His brows are arched and his fists are clenched at his sides.

"Leave Abigail alone," he growls. I'm afraid; the last thing I need right now is for Elias to make a scene. I know that he has good intentions, but I do not want any more drama at the moment.

Natalie must not have seen him coming towards us, because she seems surprised when he speaks to her. Her shock quickly fades into an icy stare.

"And who might you be?" she glares.

Elias looks like he's about to go off, but I grab onto his arm and whisper his name. He looks down at me and his eyes soften.

"Please don't," I say softly. He gives me a pleading look, but I shake my head and he seems to accept that.

"Fine, fine," he backs off and turns away from the girls. "C'mon Abby, let's go eat." He says it in a cold, flat tone, and it sends chills down my spine. I turn away too, and follow Elias towards the courtyard, tears still threatening to spill over onto my cheeks.

After a few seconds, I turn to look over my shoulder at Natalie. She's gone back to talking to her friends, a smug look on her face. I scoff to myself and continue outside to go eat lunch with my real friend.

I've fallen a little bit behind Elias because he is walking very quickly to lunch, clearly still angry. When I get outside, I see him sitting in our usual spot, looking down at his lap. I wheel myself over to him, and situate myself right next to the bench he is sitting on.

He doesn't look up at me but he knows I'm there. I don't know whether he wants to be alone or not, so I decide to at least try to strike up some form of conversation.

I take a deep breath. "Hey."

He grumbles and runs his hands through his hair before pulling his head up to look at me. He's still fuming.

"Hey, it's okay. Deep breaths Elias." I loudly inhale for a few seconds and then exhale again. He rolls his eyes but ends up joining in on the third breath. After a couple of minutes, he seems to have calmed down and is almost himself again, although he still seems kind of upset. He is staring down at his lap again, like a sad puppy dog.

I want to let him have a few seconds to himself so I take out my lunch and start to unwrap my sandwich, this is our only time to eat after all.

I have just started chewing when I think I hear Elias mumble something into his hands.

"What? Elias, did you just say something?"

He turns his head towards me but keeps it down in his hands, so that now his ear is resting against his palm. His eyes stare directly into mine.

"I'm sorry," he says, more clearly this time, although right after he utters these words, he buries his head back into his hands again, as if he's embarrassed.

This catches me off guard, I wasn't expecting him to apologize to me. I figured he would say something about Natalie, about how mean and stupid she is or something along those lines. This display of true emotion is abnormal for Elias.

He is usually so happy and smiley all the time. But in the way he is looking at me now, I can see that he's not just joking around. He actually feels terrible. And I would be lying if I said that it didn't shock me.

His eyes are red around the edges, maybe from crying, and seeing him hurt like this fills my heart with sadness.

It takes me a moment to collect my thoughts, but once I do, I try my best to cheer him up. It's the least I can do, and at this point, I just need him back to his usual, jolly self.

"Hey, hey. Elias look at me." His eyes meet mine again.

"You don't need to be sorry, for anything you did or said. I wasn't even mad at you," I say softly. "You were defending me."

He still looks unsure. "But you didn't need me there, you were doing just fine on your own and now I've probably messed everything up."

"Messed what up? From my point of view, everything had already gone in the wrong direction way before you arrived," I explain. I try to keep my tone lighthearted, so he can tell that I'm not upset with him.

He cracks a small smile, but doesn't say anything, so I keep going.

"Besides, I'm not complaining. I could use my very own knight in shining armor every once in a while," I joke, while nudging my shoulder against his. This earns a chuckle from him, and I can tell that he is already almost back to normal.

He plays along with the joke and kisses my hand before looking up at me.

"Lady Abigail, um, Abigail-" Elias stops abruptly, and whips towards me, a wild look in his eyes. He has one eyebrow raised while the other remains in its normal position. He looks ridiculous, but I can't help but wonder what prompted him to stop talking so suddenly.

He speaks again, "Wait, Abby, what the heck is your last name?" he inquires, and I laugh at the fact that he actually doesn't know. It seems like, with as well as we've gotten to know each other recently, that he would know a thing as simple as my last name. But now that I'm thinking about it, I don't think I've ever actually told him.

"It's nothing special," I start, but he interrupts me.

"Well neither is mine, I'm a Smith for god's sake," he teases, and at this, we both double over in laughter, and after a few seconds, when we come back up, I finally answer him.

"It's Bennett."

"See! That's not nearly as bad as mine!"

"Fine! But it's still not great, is it?"

"I think it's amazing."

"Well I don't like it," I resolve.

A sly grin forms on his face, as though he's thinking through a plan in his head, and I don't like this either. I sense that nothing good is going to come from this train of thought going through his head right now, yet I'm still eager to find out what it is.

"Oh come on now Elias, what're you thinking about this time?" I whine, already knowing I'm probably not going to find out just yet.

"Nothing…" He drags out the end of the word and makes his voice higher, obviously guilty of something. I want to press further, but before I get the chance, the bell rings and we both start to gather our stuff so that we can go back to class.

We end up walking together into the doors of the school and through the hallways, until we have to go our separate ways to different wings of the building.

As we pause at the intersection, I say a short goodbye to Elias, and tell him I'll see him in seventh period, but what comes next throws me off.

Elias is walking away from me backwards, waving to me as he goes. Once he gets what he assumes is a safe distance away from me, he calls out "Catch you later, Bennett!" And then swivels and jogs away quickly, obviously impressed with himself.

So that's what his plan was. I scoff as I roll myself to my classroom. He thinks he's so funny. I just hope the nickname doesn't stick.

Once I get to class, I take the first chance I can to pull out my phone and text Elias.

Abigail : What the heck was that?!

Elias : What on Earth do you mean?

So he's going to play dumb, huh?

Abigail : Deny, deny, deny, but mark my words, I will get you back someday, you'll see

Elias : And I can't wait for that day... Bennett

So it's sticking then, he's going to make sure of that. I put my phone away as class starts, but I can't focus on anything. I'm jittery because I'm so excited about physical therapy later today, and now I have Elias on my mind on top of that.

Luckily the class seems to go by quickly, and so does the next period. Before I know it, I am in my last class of the day. And you know what that means, I'm coming face to face with Elias again.

chapter 16:

Mrs. Rose teaches my seventh period science class, and although I got into that little mishap with her at the beginning of the year, we get along just fine now. I also, coincidentally, sit next to Elias in this class, just like in math, except in this classroom, we sit towards the back of the room, not front and center.

My sixth period classroom is very close to this one, so I arrive much earlier than most students, and take my usual seat, waiting for Elias. I haven't come up with a revenge plan for him yet, but I'm sure I will soon enough. I mean, how hard can it be?

I'm going through ideas in my mind when a backpack plops down in the seat next to mine, and it doesn't take long to realize who this bag belongs to. The person I've been waiting for.

Elias looks just as he usually does, as if none of the earlier events of today had even happened.

We both exchange hellos as he gets out all of his materials for this class and then sits down, so he is level with me.

"What are you doing after school today?" he eventually ends up asking.

My heart lights up again at the thought of me finally being able to go to physical therapy, so I'm excited to tell him about it.

"Actually, I have some very good news regarding that," I declare.

"Oh yeah?" he questions, scooting a little bit closer to me.

"Yep!" I reply.

"Well what is it?"

"Last week, at my appointment, your dad said that I could start physical therapy!"

His entire face lights up with joy for me.

"Really?! But I thought you were never going to be able to walk again?"

"I thought so too, and apparently so did your dad, but he said that my x-rays were looking much better than expected so he thinks, with a lot of time and effort, I should be back on my feet eventually!" I must look so gleeful, while telling him all this that

after I am done talking, he scoops me up into a tight hug.

"That's amazing Abby, I'm so happy for you!" he

congratulates, once we pull apart from the embrace. "So when do

you start then?"

"Well that's why I'm telling you, I start today, right after

school!" I smile.

"Well then, maybe I'll see you there," he winks. And

ladies and gentlemen, this is the millionth time today that Elias

Smith has caught me off guard.

"Wait, what? Why?" I give him a confused look which

makes him snicker.

"Well, it really depends on where you're going, but I

volunteer at a physical therapy center near here, and if my dad

made you an appointment, I can almost guarantee you it's the

same place. He sends all of his patients there," he explains. I

guess I can understand that, his dad is a doctor after all, it makes

sense why Elias would want to help out patients as well.

"And you just happen to be working today?" I ask.

"Yes, Miss Bennett, and I promise you, I actually had no idea that you were starting physical therapy, let alone today! But, hey, at least you'll know someone there, right?"

I roll my eyes at him for using my last name again, but he's right, it will be nice to see a familiar face there. "Fine, I guess I'll see you there then."

As soon as I finish talking, the bell sounds loudly, hushing all of the voices in the classroom and signaling the start of class.

Right when seventh period is over, I rush out of the classroom and make my way as fast as I can to my mom, who is waiting in the parking lot. I don't even say goodbye to Elias, partly because I'm just so excited, but also because I know that I will be seeing him very soon.

I practically fly through the school, before finally arriving at the front doors, where I am able to make my way down the ramp and out to the spot where Mom is. Once I am outside, I immediately spot her car, as it is relatively close to where I am. I rapidly wheel over to her, and when she spots me outside the window, she gets out of the car to help me get in and get my wheelchair into the trunk.

Once everything is situated, she scoots back into her seat and pulls out of the parking spot and into the street.

"So," she starts. "Are you excited?"

I know she's talking about physical therapy.

"I am *so* excited!" I cheer. She keeps her eyes on the road but a big smile spreads across her face. While we are driving, I tell her about Elias, and how he volunteers at the physical therapy center after school. This seems to make her relieved, as it means I will be more comfortable, and she also suggests that, because I have to go three times a week, I should just carpool with Elias after school, so that she doesn't have to come every-time. I tell her that I'll ask him about it, and this seems to please her.

I'm not lying, I will for sure ask Elias, it would be fun to hang out with him almost everyday after school.

Soon enough, we arrive at the building complex that the physical therapy place is in. Now that I'm actually here, some of my excitement is turning into nerves. What if something goes wrong and I hurt myself? What if I really did get my hopes up for nothing? What if I never get better?

But, I have to push these negative thoughts out of my head. They're just going to do more harm than good, and if I ever want things to go back to normal, I have to have a positive attitude about it, otherwise, there's no point in even trying.

Once inside the building, we check a plaque on the wall that tells us that Atlas Physical Therapy is in suite 216. We take the elevator up to the second floor, and move towards the end of the hallway. The last door on the right is the one we are looking for, so we stop, and Mom pulls it open.

We enter into a large open room, with no walls besides the exterior ones. Immediately to my left, there is a reception desk, so we head there first.

While my mom signs me in, I look around the room more. On the far right side, there are three padded tables, like the ones you see at a doctor's office, in a straight line, about ten feet apart. Behind the tables, there is a line of windows, supplying most of the light in the room. In the middle of the room, it is empty, besides the pillars being used to hold up the ceiling.

On the left wall, there are a few exercise machines and things, like yoga balls and foam rollers. Finally, just right of the door, before you get to the tables and windows, there is a small waiting-room-like space, with a few chairs and cubbies, probably to put personal belongings in.

There are only a few other people here, besides me, and the room is very quiet. As I pay closer attention to the other people's faces, I don't spot Elias anywhere. My first thought is that maybe he was wrong. Maybe Dr. Smith sent me to a different place than he usually does or something. But then I remember how we both left class at the same time, and I quickly sped out of the school as fast as I could, meaning that he probably just isn't here yet. I mean, come on, I'm on wheels. He didn't stand a chance.

Mom finishes the paperwork and we are told to go sit in the white chairs on the other side of the reception desk. We take our seats, and I scroll through my phone as we wait.

I'm more nervous than I would like to admit at this point. There are butterflies in my stomach, fluttering around. The same worries from before race through my mind. I don't know why I'm so nervous, I mean sure, it'll take a long time, but Dr. Smith seems confident that everything is going to be fine, and I trust him.

Suddenly, the door opens again, right in front of me, causing me to look up. Elias walks in through the door, and as soon as I see him, the butterflies in my stomach seem to calm down a little. At least if anything goes wrong, I know that he's here to help. I trust him too.

He doesn't notice me at first, and he goes to the front desk, probably to sign in. He scribbles something down onto a clipboard and then swivels around, his eyes scanning the room for something, or someone. Once he reaches where I am sitting, his face lights up and I shyly wave at him. He flashes me one of his award winning smiles and takes a couple steps forward, plopping down in the chair next to me.

Mom notices him now too, and she looks up from the article she is reading on her phone.

"Hello Abby!" Elias nods at me. He turns to my mom. "And you must be Mrs. Bennett?" he asks politely.

She smiles from ear to ear, "That I am. And I assume you are the famous Elias Smith." A bright pink creeps up into my cheeks. Hopefully he didn't pay close attention to what Mom said.

Elias chuckles and holds his right hand out to shake my mom's. "Well, I don't know about famous, but you got the rest right."

"Oh, trust me, you're a celebrity in our house. Abigail talks about you all of the time!"

Elias looks right at me, eyes widened, with a clear look of amusement written all over his face. I blush even more furiously which causes him to look more delighted.

"Mom..." I groan, burying my head in my hands.

"Oh wow Abby! I'm flattered!" he jokes. Then he leans down to whisper in my ear, "Don't worry, I talk about you plenty as well." I snap my head up, but before I can respond, he tells my mom he has to get to work and walks away, a clear bounce in his step, that wasn't there before. Leaving me, sitting speechless with a bright red face, dumbfounded.

chapter 17:

"He seems nice!" my mom notes.

I silently nod in agreement.

It's not much longer before someone comes to get us to see the physical therapist. I am shown over to the first padded table, and both Mom and the assistant help me get up, so that I am sitting on the table.

It is then that the therapist finally comes over. The first thing that I notice about her is how kind she looks. She looks to be about my mom's age, with slightly curled blonde hair and blue eyes. She's wearing a little bit of makeup, but not too much that it's inappropriate in any way.

She walks directly over to me and shakes my hand first, and then my mother's.

When she speaks, I am shocked to hear a British accent lacing her words. "Hello there Abigail! I'm Samantha Hewitt, but you can just call me Sam if you'd like," she greets, smiling.

"Nice to meet you!" I bubble.

She starts talking to me a little bit about the process of what we're going to be doing in our time together. She explains that we will begin with some small toe strengthening exercises, and then gradually move up to use more and more of my legs.

She then instructs me to take my shoes off, which I do, and lifts my feet so that they are up on the table.

"Can you wiggle your toes at all yet?" she inquires.

I've actually never tried, I just assumed I wouldn't be able to so I never really thought about it.

"I'm not sure," I say shyly, slightly embarrassed that I don't know.

"That's alright! How about we try together?" she encourages. Then she counts me down, "3...2...1...and go!"

I look down at my feet, and try to focus on putting all of my energy into moving my toes, even just the tiniest bit.

I struggle for a few seconds, but then, seemingly out of nowhere, one of my toes twitches.

I look up, mouth gaping open, and my mom and Sam are beaming at me.

"Great job Abigail!" Sam cheers.

I feel proud of myself, and with this newfound courage, I try again and again, each time, moving my toes more and more until, after about fifteen minutes, I can wiggle them all, at least a little bit.

Sam seems very impressed with my progress and gives me a high five to show it.

She then explains how she will spend a few minutes during each session massaging the muscles in my feet with a special tool. I think that it's supposed to help loosen up my muscles, since they haven't been active in so long. She gets to work and I relax while she works her magic.

I keep looking over at my mom, who is repeatedly checking the time on her watch impatiently.

"Hey Mom?" I ask.

She looks up from her watch. "What is it sweetie?"

"Do you have something else you need to do right now?"

"Oh, no, it's just that today's my day to drive Alex's soccer carpool, and to be honest, I thought that this appointment would be shorter. I just don't want to be late," she replies. "But I will stay with you as long as you need me," she adds.

"All done!" Sam pipes.

"Oh! That's perfect timing then! Are we all good to go?" my mom asks her.

Sam looks apologetic, she must have heard our conversation. "I'm sorry but not quite yet. Abigail needs to learn some exercises that she can practice at home in between visits. During every appointment she will meet with me and then work with one of my exercise therapists."

Mom sighs. "Alright, of course."

We hurry over to the other side of the studio, where all of the equipment is set up. I can see Elias, standing in a corner, looking over a sheet of paper with another woman. She seems to be a little younger than my mom, probably somewhere in her early thirties, and she has bright red hair that is straight and shoulder length. She also has bangs that fall onto her forehead at the perfect spot. I've never been able to pull off bangs, but this woman certainly can.

Sam calls her over and both she and Elias quickly walk over to us. Elias shoots me a grin and winks at me, causing my cheeks to grow warm again, just as they did earlier, and all of my confidence from a few minutes ago gets flushed right down the drain.

Sam starts her introductions, "Abigail, this is Lili and Elias, although it seems as if you already know the latter," Sam comments, obviously taking note of our exchange.

I shake hands with Lili and mutter a 'nice to meet you', feeling very self-conscious, but she still gives me a warm grin, so I think I'm going to like her.

"Lili works here full time, and Elias just kind of follows her around, helping out with whatever needs to be done," Sam continues. They both nod in agreement with Sam and before I know it, introductions are over and Sam has gone to meet with another patient.

Before we start, I look over at my mom again and see that she is still hastily checking her watch, over and over again.

But before I can mention it, she does.

"Hey Elias? Do you think that you could give Abigail a ride home? I have something I need to do and I'm going to be late, so it would be really helpful if-"

He cuts her off, "Of course Mrs. Bennett! I would be happy to." he responds politely. "I just have to finish my shift here, but that shouldn't take too long should it Lili?"

She shakes her head, "Don't worry about it Elias, you can leave early today."

"Awesome! Go do whatever you need to do Mrs. Bennett, I promise I'll get Abby home, safe and sound," he assures, sneaking a glance at me.

"Thank you so much, Elias. You are a lifesaver," and with that, she starts to speed walk towards the door. "I'll see you when you get home Abigail!" She blows a kiss over her shoulder to me, and I return the favor before waving until she is out of sight. I can't say that I'm too happy about this arrangement, but it should be fine, as long as Elias doesn't pull any more stunts on me.

Lili claps her hands together and I snap back to the task at hand.

"Alright then! Let's get started!"

It doesn't take too long until I'm done with Lili and Elias. All they have to do is show me a few exercises to do with my toes, which are basically just different combinations of lifting certain toes up and down. I'm supposed to do them every morning and every night, in order to get the strength in my feet back up.

Once we are done, Lili bids us farewell and moves on to another patient, while Elias waits for me to put my shoes back on and get myself situated.

"Ready?" he asks, as I am finishing tying up my second shoe.

"Ready," I confirm, and he holds the door open while I wheel out into the hallway. As we are making our way to the elevators, he starts up a conversation.

"So, Bennett, how was your first physical therapy appointment? Everything you had dreamed and hoped it would be?" he teases.

I play along, "Oh, it was everything I had dreamt of and more!" We both laugh.

He turns more serious, although he still has a light hearted tone in his voice. "For real though, did everything go okay?"

"Yeah, it actually did. I didn't know I was even able to move my toes, so that was new to me. And everybody there is so nice."

"They really are, Lili is my favorite person there, she's super chill. You're lucky you got her, and me, as your exercise therapists." He smiles at himself for the little 'and me' he added in there. We are now at the elevators.

I resume the joking conversation. "Are you sure I'm lucky to have you there?"

"100% sure, I'm the best person you know, admit it. You think I'm the most hilarious, smartest, most awesome guy in the whole wide world."

"Oh, don't flatter yourself Elias, I can swap you out for any other guy at the school and I wouldn't miss you one bit."

He giggles and we roll out into the parking lot where he leads me to his car. When we get there, I think it's going to be awkward trying to get me and then my wheelchair into the car, but he picks me up in one swift movement and places me in the passenger seat. It surprises me that he knows exactly what to do, even when it comes to folding the chair up and stacking it in the trunk. Even my mom still has problems with it sometimes.

I make a mental note to ask him about it later as he climbs into the driver's seat and shuts the door behind him.

He starts the car and buckles his seatbelt over his lap. He looks over at me, making sure I do the same.

He then hands me his phone. "Put your address into Google Maps so we don't get lost," he instructs, and I do as I'm told, before handing the phone back to him. He props it up on a mount he has on his dashboard so that it's easy to see, and puts the car in reverse to back out of the parking spot.

We drive in a comfortable silence for a short while. The radio is playing very quietly in the background, but even so, it can barely be heard. I'm not used to this. Usually when I drive anywhere with friends, we either turn up the music to a really loud volume, or we chat the whole ride. But I think I kind of like the stillness, it's peaceful.

Elias interrupts the quiet. "Oh!" he exclaims, like he had forgotten I was here in the first place. "You can change the music to whatever you want, I don't really care, as long as it's not country," he grins.

I let out a little laugh. "Don't worry, I would never even dream of liking country music."

"That's good, because if you did, I think I would have to stop hanging out with you."

"Hey now! I thought that we had already decided that *you're* replaceable to *me*, so I think it would be *I* who would stop hanging out with *you*!"

We fell right back into our back and forth banter, just as we had earlier.

He stays quiet for a minute, clearly pondering his response. "Are you sure about that Abby? You wanna know what I think?"

I playfully roll my eyes. "No actually. Please spare me from what goes on inside that wonky head of yours," I tease.

He takes his eyes off the road for just a second to make a pouty face at me, but then turns back quickly. "Meanie," he whines. "Well, I'm going to tell you anyway," he states.

"*I* think that you secretly love hanging out with me and you'll never trade me out for anyone," he smiles.

I scoff. "Not true!"

"It *is* true, you just won't admit it to yourself!"

"Nope!" I say stubbornly.

"Oh come on Abigail! Just say it! You like having me around."

"Fine!" I raise my hands up in defeat. "I enjoy hanging out with you, is that what you want to hear?" I scrunch my nose up at him.

He smirks, clearly feeling proud of himself, while keeping his eyes on the road ahead of us. I recognize where we are, we're not far from my house, no more than a few minutes away.

Elias opens his mouth to say something else but I interject before he has the chance.

"But I swear Elias, if you press this anymore I will break up with you on the spot!"

Immediately after I say it, I regret it, but it's too late.

Elias's eyes widen, while a huge smile spreads across his face.

I bury my head into my hands, heat rushing up to my cheeks. I can't see where his eyes are as I am looking down at my lap, but I feel his arm reach out and ruffle my hair, messing it up.

"Break up? Aw, Abby, that's so cute! But I didn't know that we were a couple," he jokes, clearly enjoying this.

"Oh shut up, Elias. You know what I meant," I murmur into my palms.

He chuckles again but doesn't say anything for a few more seconds. I lift my head up to face him again, and he seems to take notice of my pink cheeks.

"Ha! I made you blush!" he jests.

This makes my cheeks flush an even brighter red.

I turn my face towards the window and cover my cheeks with the palms of my hands.

"It wouldn't be the first time today," I mumble under my breath, remembering the time at physical therapy earlier.

I say it to myself but he must hear me, as he responds with an amused, "Oh, trust me, I know."

I whip around in my seat and lightly shove Elias' arm, in between his elbow and shoulder.

"Hey!" he gasps. "You can't hit the driver! I could have crashed the car!" he complains, being the drama queen that he is.

He tries to imitate the face that I made earlier, scrunching up his nose at me, which makes me start to laugh uncontrollably. I double over giggling, and when I pull my head back up, Elias is just pulling up to my driveway.

I quickly gather myself as the car rolls to a stop. Elias puts the car into park and then immediately gets out and moves around to the trunk, grabbing my wheelchair and unfolding it before bringing it back to me.

I watch him in the rearview mirror as he does this. It's so odd that he knows exactly what to do. I mean, I guess it could just be because of his dad, but getting that chair in and out of the car is no easy task. He must have had some other experience with it, and I struggle to think of what it could be. I wondered if he was ever in an accident and needed to use a wheelchair. I really do want to ask him about it, but maybe it's personal and I don't want to push it.

He closes the trunk and brings the wheelchair around to my door, which I have already opened. I am sitting with my legs dangling out the side of the car, so it's easier for him to lift me out.

When he reaches me, I give him a little smile and he returns the favor. He gracefully lifts me up and softly places me back down in my wheelchair. Once I am out of the way, he shuts the car door and locks it.

"Wait, Elias, why did you lock your car, aren't you going home?"

"I'll leave in a minute, I want to make sure you get inside safely first," he replies, grinning at me.

"I am perfectly capable of getting myself inside my own home, there aren't even any stairs!" I argue.

"Alright then, go ahead!" he teases, gesturing towards my house.

I let out a little "hmph" and scoot myself towards the garage door. It takes me a few seconds just to make my way up the rest of the driveway because it is so slanted, but I eventually make it up to the top and move toward the keypad where I have to enter in the code.

I reach up as high as I can, trying to reach the buttons but no such luck. I keep trying over and over again, but finally look back down the driveway in defeat.

I turn back to Elias's car and see that he hasn't left yet, he is just leaning against the hood and staring at me, with his arms crossed on his chest and a smug look on his face.

I glare at him. "Elias, please come help me," I say through gritted teeth.

"What was that? I thought you just asked for my help, but I clearly remember-"

"Elias just get over here now or I'll change my mind!" I beckon.

He jogs over to me and asks me what the code is. I quickly tell him and he punches it in. The garage door opens right on cue and I lead him through the garage and towards the door that goes into my house.

Elias steps in front of me to open the door and he holds it open while I wheel into my house.

Once in the kitchen, I check the clock. Mom should be back any minute now.

"You guys have a nice house," Elias comments, looking all around him at the living room and kitchen.

"Thanks!" I respond.

He points to the staircase on our right. "Although, I'm guessing those aren't too fun in your current condition," he jokes.

I let out a small chuckle. "Are you kidding? I love not getting to go upstairs without the help of an entire army!" I say sarcastically, which causes us both to laugh.

He stops laughing, eyes darting down to his watch, and mumbles "oh shoot" as if he just remembered he's late for something.

He looks back up at me. "I'm so sorry Abby but I promised my mom and dad that I would make dinner tonight, and I still have to go to the grocery store. Will you be okay here alone for a while?" He rubs the back of his neck and there is guilt laced into his voice, like he doesn't want to leave, but I assure him he has nothing to worry about.

"Of course! My mom should be home soon anyway. Go do what you have to do!" I convince him.

He smiles before leaning down to give a short hug.

"Just go out the way I came in?" he questions.

I nod and he turns back around, waving to me as he walks out into the garage.

Once the door closes behind him, I can't seem to wipe the smile off of my face. I roll over right next to the couch, and since I can't lift myself onto the sofa itself, I stay in my wheelchair right beside it and turn on the TV.

The rest of the night passes by rapidly. My mom arrives home and soon after, my dad finishes work. Once Alex gets home from practice we eat dinner together, watch a show, and then go to bed.

chapter 18:

It has been three weeks since my first physical therapy appointment. I currently go three times a week, after school on Mondays, Wednesdays, and Fridays. Each day is just as exciting as the first.

Elias is there every time. It could just be a coincidence that his shifts are at the same time as my appointments, but with Elias, I wouldn't be surprised if that wasn't actually the case. After I told mom how much fun I had when Elias had given me a ride home on the first day, she asked him if he could drive me both from school to the physical therapy building, and also home afterwards.

Of course he said he would love to, so I've been spending a lot more time with him lately. Things are going exceptionally well with my legs. I am now up to being able to control my toes, feet, and even ankles! I know that even when my movement is back to normal, I will still have a hard time walking. It will take a while to build my muscle strength back up, but I'm still so happy with the pace that everything is moving at, and I am hopeful for the future.

I still haven't talked to Natalie since the incident at school. She doesn't even glare at me in the hallways anymore, she just ignores me completely.

My heart breaks every-time I see her, as I remember how close we've been our entire lives. I don't even care that she was mean to me, I thought that our friendship meant more to her than that. Obviously I was wrong.

I have tried to text her a few times, but she always reads it and doesn't respond. When I talk to Elias about her, he says that she's not worth it, and that I should just stop trying. Maybe he's right and it's best to sever all contact with her, but I don't know if I can do that.

It's now Friday night, and I am sitting in bed, thinking about the events of the past few weeks. Even though the Natalie situation is bad, nearly everything else in my life is going well, which makes me cheerful.

I'm so happy it's the weekend; getting up early for school everyday is exhausting, so I'm excited to be able to sleep late tomorrow.

Plus, the fact that it's Friday means that Halloween is only a week away. I haven't figured out what I'm doing for the holiday yet, as I would usually go to some exclusive party with Natalie and my other ex-friends. Maybe I'll ask Elias if he has any plans yet.

My eyelids start to get heavy and feel like they are about to fall. I am ready to turn off my light and go to sleep when I hear a soft *ding* coming from my phone that is charging on my nightstand.

I pick it up and immediately smile at the contact name.

Elias : Heyyyyy Abby. U still awake?
Abigail : Maybe

Elias : I'm going to take that as a yes :)

I roll my eyes.

Elias : I have a question for you

Abigail : Ask away

Elias : Okay so I have tickets to go see a movie with my dad tomorrow afternoon, but apparently he forgot about some work thing he has to go to...

Abigail : And...?

Elias : Will you come with me?

Abigail : Depends, what's the movie?

Elias : Ummmm... You can't judge, okay?

Abigail : Eliasssss

Elias : Promise!

Abigail : Fine! I promise, what is it?

Elias : It's just this old rom com that looked funny

Abigail : Elias! You were going to go see a rom com with your dad?!

Elias : Hey! You said you wouldn't judge

Abigail : I'm not! I LOVE rom coms, what movie is it?

Elias : Pretty Woman

Abigail : Yessss! Good choice, I'm in. What time are you picking me up?

Elias : The movie starts at 3:00 so I was thinking around 2:15?

Abigail : Sounds good! I'll see you then, goodnight Elias!

Elias : Goodnight Bennett

Abigail : >:(

Elias : :)

I put my phone face down on my nightstand before going to sleep, although I am not nearly as tired anymore. I'm so excited for tomorrow! I think it's going to be a lot of fun to hang out with Elias outside of my mandatory activities, like school and physical therapy. We talk when he drives me around, but that usually only lasts a few minutes.

I slowly drift off to sleep, thinking about tomorrow and all it will bring.

By the time I wake up the next morning, it's already eleven. I sit up groggily and reach for my phone. The screen lights up with a text from a certain someone.

Elias : See you soon! :)

I smile at the message but don't feel the need to respond, so I text my family instead, letting my mom and dad know that I'm awake. It's no more than a minute before Mom bustles into my room to say good morning.

She gives me a quick kiss on the cheek before gliding over to my closet, ready to help me pick out an outfit for the day. I've never understood why Mom is always so rushed in the morning. She's always been that way, even if we don't have anywhere to be.

As she is rifling through my clothes, she speaks over her shoulder at me.

"So Abby, have any plans today?" She asks me this every weekend, kind of as a light hearted joke, as I usually don't go anywhere besides school and doctors appointments anymore.

I'm about to automatically say no, but then I remember the movie with Elias.

"Actually I do!" I exclaim. This causes her to flip around towards me, a look of shock on her face, which quickly melts into a smile.

"That's great honey! What are you doing? Do you need a ride or anything?" she questions, clearly interested to hear more.

"Elias asked me if I wanted to go see a movie with him this afternoon. He got tickets with his dad but apparently there was some last minute work thing he had to go to so he bailed. And no, I don't need a ride, Elias is picking me up around 2:15," I explain. She claps her hands and turns back to my closet.

"We need to pick out what you're wearing then! This is your first time hanging out with a friend in months!"

I shoot a playful glare to her back at the slight dig but she can't see me anyway so I move on.

I decide to only eat a small lunch, as I figure I will get some sort of snack at the theater later. Everyone seems very happy that I am actually going out and doing something today, which makes me feel even more excited.

Before I know it, Elias is texting me saying that he is on his way over to my house.

I wait by the door, anxious for him to get here while my mom stands next to me, clearly jittery as well. Although she would never admit it, I think her original enthusiasm and happiness have worn off and now she's getting more nervous for me.

We both just stand at the door in silence until we hear a loud knock echoing through the entire house.

Immediately I swing open the door and see Elias standing with his hand still in midair.

He lets his hand drop down to his side while flashing me his usual toothy grin before smiling up at my mother as well.

"Good afternoon Mrs. Bennett!" he greets her.

"Good afternoon Elias!" she responds, matching his contagious smile with one of her own.

They chat for a few minutes, with Elias explaining his plans to her and reassuring her that he will be extra careful with me. I know he does this to try to calm her nerves, but I also know that there is nothing anyone can do to stop my mom from worrying about me, it's just the way she is.

I clear my throat and give Mom a look that is clearly meant to be a signal for her to stop asking questions and just let us leave already, and although she looks reluctant, she takes the hint and backs off.

With a quick "have fun!" and a few waves, Elias and I are off and on our way to the theater.

The drive is short and easy, with a few jokes and witty comments exchanged before we arrive at our destination.

He helps me out of his car with ease, and together we head towards the doors of the movie theater.

It is an unusually warm, sunny day, especially considering the fact that it is already well into fall.

Right in front of the large black doors, there is a circle of benches surrounding a large fountain where some younger children are sitting while tossing coins into the pool of water.

As we are nearing the fountain, Elias stops walking and turns to me.

"Why don't you just chill here for a minute while I go grab the tickets?" he suggests.

I agree and watch as he jogs towards the ticket counter and speaks to the employee occupying the window.

While he is talking, I notice that a small frown has started to form on Elias's face, and I briefly wonder what could be wrong, but it's not long before he turns and jogs back to me.

As soon as he reaches where I am, I question him in order to figure out what is going on. "Hey, what happened? Is there something wrong with the tickets?" I inquire.

He just shakes his head before saying, "No, it's just that I apparently forgot to tell my dad that you had agreed to come with me today, so he canceled the tickets." He sounds disappointed, but I'm not too sad about it, it doesn't mean that we can't still hang out for a little while.

"Oh no! I was totally looking forward to seeing Julia Roberts! It's alright though, Elias. We can find something else to do, it's not the end of the world," I say, trying to get him to perk up, and, fortunately, it works, putting a joyous expression back on his face. I swear, the mood changes this boy has are going to drive me crazy.

"Okay!" he exclaims. "So, what do you want to do?"

I think for a second, but my head draws up empty. "I don't know, any ideas?"

He is silent for a minute, but then I can practically see the light bulb pop into his head.

"We could go get frozen yogurt?" he suggests, and I am immediately on board.

"Yes!" I yell, clearly very excited. Multiple people around us shoot me an annoyed glance, but this just causes us both to laugh uncontrollably, resulting in even more glares.

After we finally catch our breath, Elias leads the way as we walk towards Yoguz frozen yogurt. It's right around the corner from the theater so it's not long until we arrive at our destination.

Elias, being the gentleman he is, opens the glass doors for me on the way into the store, and I quickly thank him before I rush inside. Once on the other side of the threshold, my senses fill with sweetness as I take in my surroundings. All of the vibrant colors, all of the candy toppings, the entire wall of frozen yogurt dispensers, I can practically taste it already.

Suddenly I hear a certain someone chuckling right next to me. I look up and see Elias holding his hand over his mouth, trying to stifle a laugh.

I punch his arm, getting his attention. "Hey!" I whine. "What're you laughing at?"

"You should've seen your face when we came in! You were like-" he opens his eyes wide and sticks his tongue out the side of his mouth, like a dog drooling over it's favorite toy. I gasp, offended.

"That is definitely NOT what my face looked like!"

"Yep, you looked exactly like that!"

"Did not!"

"Did too!"

We went back and forth a few more times until we both simultaneously seemed to realize that we were in a public place.

I look around the store, and although there are no other customers besides us, there is one employee at the counter looking like she is trying her hardest not to laugh at us.

As we walk over to pick out our frozen yogurt flavors, no one says anything. Now that both of us are aware of the presence of another person, the chatter has gone silent. I can hear some pop songs playing through the speakers in the ceiling, but it's pretty quiet and I can't make out exactly what it is.

We swirl our favorite flavors, mine cake batter and Elias' chocolate, into our cups until the bowls are practically overflowing, and then move on to toppings. I kept it simple with some gummy bears and a cherry, but Elias scoops some of almost everything onto his. Sprinkles, gummy bears, nerds, cookie dough bites, marshmallows, and so much more! It looks like one of those characters from the Candy Crush game has puked sweets all over his frozen yogurt.

We pay for our Yoguz and, since the weather is so nice, decide to sit at one of the small tables outside. As we settle down at the metal table, Elias pulls out his phone.

"What're you doing?" I ask, confused because he never really goes on his phone while we're hanging out.

He simply shrugs and replies, "I thought we could take a selfie, you know? As like a memory?"

"Oh, yeah, sure!" I nod.

He holds his phone up in the air and I lean closer to him, across the table, so that we can both get into the shot. We hold up our food and smile. I make sure I hear the snapping sound of the camera before I move back to my side of the table and turn to face Elias again. We start to eat our frozen yogurt, and my first bite tastes like heaven.

"That's so cute! Can you send it to me?" I request through a mouth full of cold, delicious sweetness.

Almost immediately, my phone buzzes and I check it to see the photo we just took. I absolutely love it.

"Do you mind if I post this on my Instagram?" I question, making sure Elias is fine with it before I post anything.

"Of course!" he exclaims. "Let all of your old friends see that I'm your bestie now!" he says proudly.

I roll my eyes. "Ok sounds good, 'bestie'. You sure are confident for someone I've barely known for a month."

He sticks his tongue out at me and I do the same in return before turning back to my phone in order to add the photo to my profile.

I haven't posted a single picture since everything happened, but I used to obsess about my social media page. Trying to come up with the perfect poses, the perfect captions, the perfect profile in order to get the most likes and comments. But this time, I don't spend any time on that. I just quickly add the photo to my feed and tag Elias, not even caring enough to add a caption.

chapter 19:

I jerk awake, my eyes darting around to check my surroundings. I am already standing up straight, staring at my reflection in my bathroom mirror, but something is wrong. It doesn't take long for me to realize that I am back to that life changing night of a few months ago. Standing in my bathroom, staring at myself in the mirror. Standing up on my own two legs, my hair perfectly curled, wearing a pale pink crop top with light blue ripped jeans. Despite the turmoil going on in my head, I unwillingly smile at myself and then turn to run downstairs.

In my mind, I know what's about to happen. I remember this night perfectly. I know that I will never get to attend the party I am heading to. But my body doesn't seem to want to listen.

I have the same conversation with my mom, exchange the same texts with Natalie, jump into her car when I see it in the driveway.

I am yelling at myself to stop. Stop driving in the car, stop moving forward, stop the inevitable from happening, but I can't. I am trapped.

Everything goes by in the exact way I remember it and although my mouth is chatting excitedly, I feel a sense of dread consuming my emotions.

When we pull up outside of Daisy's house, my heart drops to the floor. She smiles at me and asks if she can sit in the passenger seat. And for a second, I'm just happy to see her. But then I remember how the rest of this dream is going to play out.

"NO!" I try to scream. But no sound comes out. My body somehow cheerfully says sure. No, no, no. I can't let this happen again. I can't. There's no way.

My body carries me to the back of the car. I have no choice. I keep trying to scream, over and over again.

The bright lights and honking. It's here. It's happening. I let out one final scream, which this time seems to get through the barrier between my mind and my body.

When the impact happens, I jolt awake. I sit up straight in my bed, panting loudly, eyes skimming the room for any danger, but there is none. I check the digital clock on my nightstand. 2:36am.

I put my hand over my chest and try to steady my breath. I hear quick footsteps moving towards my door and it opens. My dad rushes over to my side and turns on the lamp next to my bed.

"Abby? Oh thank god, you're okay. I heard screaming, did something happen?" he asks, concerned.

"Just a bad dream," I answer sheepishly, feeling bad for waking him up in the middle of the night.

His eyes look sad. "The accident?" he whispers.

I just silently nod and he says nothing. He gives me a big bear hug and I hug him back, burying my face into his neck. A few tears escape my eyes and trickle down my face and onto Dad's shirt.

We stay like that for a few moments. I think he knows that I don't really feel like talking about it because the entire time neither of us say anything.

Once I stop crying, he pulls away and I wipe the stray tears from my face.

He asks if I'm okay and I tell him yes before he leaves my bedroom so that I can go back to sleep. After the door softly closes, I flop back down onto my pillow and try to fall back asleep, with no luck.

After a few minutes of failing to shut my mind down, I open my phone, deciding that maybe scrolling through social media might help me calm down.

The first thing I see when I open the Instagram app is all of the notifications from my post with Elias on Saturday. There are a lot of people who made nice comments, complimenting my hair, or outfit. I am going through and liking all of the sweet words, when one specific person catches my eye. *Natalie.*

Hers is the only comment that isn't polite, but mean instead.

nataliemiller02 : don't let these other comments fool you, sweet Abigail. you are a freak. no one likes you, and no one ever will.

I don't know how to react. On one hand, I am trying to ignore Natalie and all that she stands for. I never thought that our friendship was toxic before, but it is apparent to me now. On the other hand, something deep inside of me longs for us to be friends again. I know that I shouldn't care about what she is saying about me, but a part of me doesn't want to let go, to truly believe that our friendship is done forever.

A few tears come to my eyes, and I don't make an effort to hold them back. I report the comment, so it will be gone by the morning, but that doesn't erase the effects of her words on my heart.

I look through all of my previous posts on my feed. The most recent one besides the one from yesterday, is one of Natalie, Daisy, and I on the first day of school.

I remember we all drove to the building together that morning, huddled in Natalie's car together. We were annoyed to be going back to school, but excited for the year to come. We were juniors now, and the three of us were just glad to be upperclassmen. The actual photo of us is one that Jake, who Natalie had a crush on at the time, took of us. The three of us are standing in front of our school with our arms around each other and looking radiant in the bright morning sun.

The other photos are the kind of thing you would expect to see on a sixteen year old's social media page. A picture of Natalie and I at the beach, posing in our swimsuits. One of me on a hike with my family. A couple are of Daisy and I, smiling and laughing together like we used to do.

But my mind keeps coming back to the one snapshot from the first day of school. I was in such a different mindset then. I had a large group of friends, I was invited to every party, I didn't care about academics. To put it plainly, I was a typical mean girl. I remember tripping that Freshman in the hallway. I was a bully. I was not nice and I treated other people the way Natalie is treating me now.

I thought that she was the one who changed after the accident, but really she's the same as she's always been, a mean girl. And I'm now on the receiving side of it.

I know now that I'm the one that's changed. I really believe that this entire situation and hanging out with Elias has made me a better person. But the question is, would I have changed if not for the accident? Would I have ever realized that my actions were unacceptable? Or would I still be a cliche popular mean girl today. I shudder at the thought. I genuinely hope not.

Monday morning I wake up (way too early might I add) to the non stop *beep beep beep* of my alarm, and I am not particularly delighted to realize that I have school again today. However, on the bright side, I do have physical therapy this afternoon. Some people may see this as a burden, but I'm happy to do anything that will help me get back to being fully myself.

My morning routine passes by in a blur, and soon I find myself back at Stonebrook High School, feeling as though only a moment has gone by since I was sleeping in my sweet, soft bed. Oh how I wish I could be back there right now.

I wheel into the school building as usual, tuning out the chaos ensuing around me. You know how it is in the mornings before school starts, loud chatter, a few skateboards, quite a bit of yelling, it's the norm.

I sit by the elevator doors, willing them to open as soon as possible so that I can get to my class without having to deal with any small talk or questions. I've been back at school for a while now, but I still get a few stares here and there, and although I get that they're not trying to be rude, it still bugs me.

Luckily, almost as soon as I press the button, the lift arrives, not many people using it I guess. I smoothly roll inside, and press the button with the number two on it. The button lights up, which is satisfying to me.

The doors whoosh closed and the small area is plunged into silence, blocking out all of the ruckus from the lobby. I breathe a sigh of relief, and brace myself for the short ascent up to the second floor.

I move out into the hallway and immediately focus on getting through the crowd of students to my classroom. Through the blur of blue lockers and brightly colored clothing, I see Daisy's locker out of the corner of my eye. The school has kept the small memorial up at her locker, as I'm guessing no one wants to be the first to suggest taking it down. I make the conscious decision to move past it quickly. I don't have the time or energy right now to think about everything that has happened.

I make it to Mr. Carson's class five minutes before the bell rings, so there are only a few students already in their seats. I look back towards my desk and see that Elias is already here as well.

He's sitting in his chair with his head down on the table, using his right arm as a pillow. His long, curly hair is spilling over the sleeve of his white hoodie, and he looks so peaceful, it almost pains me to disturb him.

I wheel myself to our desk and wait for him to startle awake. When he doesn't, I gently rub his arm and say his name just above a whisper.

His back straightens and he jerks awake so suddenly that I have to lean backwards in order to avoid getting smacked in the head. His face looks terrified, but when he looks my way his facial features soften once again, and a large grin lights up his face.

"Oh! Thank goodness it's you Bennett, you scared the crap out of me," he says, but it's muffled by his hands, which are rubbing his eyes vigorously, as if he's trying hard to wake himself up.

"Sorry!" I apologize. "But I had to get you up somehow, class is about to start." More students are now filing into the classroom, and it is about seventy five percent full. "Anyway, why were you asleep in the first place?"

"I'm so tired Abby, I just could not fall asleep at all last night. Maybe it was because it was Sunday or something, I really don't know." His happy demeanor falters for a second, and he does look exhausted, but he snaps out of it quickly, the smile returning to his face. "How did you sleep?"

"Oh, pretty much the same, probably for a similar reason too, I can never fall asleep on Sunday nights." He nods in agreement, and makes himself busy by getting his supplies for this class out from his backpack.

Thinking back to last night makes my stomach churn. First the dream, and then Natalie's comment, it did take a toll on me, and I'm guessing that I look pretty sleepy too. I checked this morning, and the comment was gone, so at least I don't have to think about it again. I wasn't going to tell Elias about it, because I knew he would probably just get all defensive and try to confront Natalie again, but if he was awake too, there is a high chance that he saw it himself.

He's still piling his notebooks onto the table when I interrupt. "Hey Elias?" I question.

He turns to look at me, wondering what I'm about to say next. "Yeah?"

I rip the band-aid off. "Did you happen to see Natalie's comment on my post last night?"

His expression clouds slightly, and although he tries not to show it, I can tell he is angry. "I did," he responds shortly. "I had forgotten about that but I definitely saw it. You shouldn't listen to her, you know? People definitely like you, she's just jealous that you've found new friends."

I smile at him. "Don't worry, I can assure you that I know all of those things. I'm okay, alright?"

His concern fades as fast as it came. "Alright, Abby. I'll leave it be, but please don't let her get to you, okay?"

"I won't, promise." I hold out my pinky finger, to make a point.

He grins and wraps his finger around mine. The bell

rings, and it is time to start boring calculus.

chapter 20:

"Yes, Abby! That's incredible!" Sam is cheering at me. I look around at the other people in the office, my cheeks are turning red from embarrassment by her outward display of praise. I am at physical therapy once again, honestly this place is starting to feel as familiar as school, and Sam is clearly very happy with my progress. I can move my ankles in full circles now, and I am currently using a superhuman amount of focus to try to contract my calf muscles. It takes a lot of work and concentration, but obviously Sam is proud of me regardless.

The more I have gotten to know Sam, the more I like her. She is always amazingly nice to me, and I constantly feel like I am improving when I'm around her.

"Alrighty then, I feel like we've made a lot of progress today! Are you ready to go see Lili?" I smile and nod in response. Sam helps lift me off the table and back into my wheelchair, so

192

that I don't have to do it myself, and then we move over to the exercise area of the room.

Elias is here too, as usual, and he is currently helping Lili with another patient. Sam stands to wait with me while they finish up, and I look down at my lap and play with my fingers.

No more than thirty seconds later, a familiar voice makes me perk back up.

"Abbyyyyyy!" Elias yells as he sees me waiting. He runs over and scoops me up into a ginormous hug. This boy, I swear. The last time I saw him was probably less than twenty minutes ago, but he still acts like he hasn't seen me in years.

"Elias!" I chuckle and pat his back while he still has his arms wrapped around me. "We literally drove here together!"

He mumbles something that sounds like "So what?" into my shoulder before releasing me and pulling back. I smile up at him to let him know that I'm not seriously mad at him and then look around his arm at Sam and Lili. It seems like they are talking over some exercises for me to try today, so I probably have a little bit more time until we get started.

I am trying to come up with a short conversation topic for Elias and I, when I remember that this weekend is Halloween!

Elias is still staring off into the distance so I call his name to get his attention. He immediately turns back to me, flashing his trademark smile and showing that he is listening to what I have to say.

"What's up?" he asks.

"I was just wondering if you had any plans for Halloween this weekend?" He seems to ponder this for a minute, but then shakes his head.

"I don't think so, my dad has to work late that night so I'm guessing nothing's really happening in my family. Why do you ask?" And from the look on his face, I can tell he is hoping he knows why.

"Well I was just wondering if you wanted to hang out?" I question, slightly worried that he will say no.

He seems to enjoy seeing me squirm, and makes a big show of pretending to think about it. He chuckles at himself, and then responds, "Of course, Abby!"

I breathe a sigh of relief. "Alright then!"

Noticing that Lili and Sam seem to be about done talking, I wrap up the conversation. "Want to text about the details later?"

"Sounds good!"

Lili is making her way over to us now, and Elias tries to put his "serious" face on. However, even when he works his hardest he can't really hide the grin that always creeps back up.

We get to work on my exercises for the day, which are nothing really outside the usual. Toe stretches, ankle strengthening, and some new things to help the muscles in my calves start to come back.

I schedule my next appointment, and sit for a while to wait until Elias is done helping Lili with a few other patients. It doesn't take much time, and soon enough, I'm already in Elias's car, driving back to my house.

The usual road we take is closed due to construction, so we have to take a small detour, and we end up on the same road where the accident happened. We're traveling the other direction, sure, but so far, my parents have gone out of their way to make sure we haven't driven down here at all since that day.

I know that Elias probably has no idea, as his mood has not changed, but I am struggling to keep my breath in check as waves of nerves and other unidentifiable feelings wash over my body. Although I may look calm on the outside, my insides are going through immense turmoil, and I don't know how much longer I can keep my composure.

My breathing gets heavier and more ragged, but Elias still hasn't noticed, and is bopping his head along to the song that is playing on the radio.

Then we pass Daisy's house. It goes by in a blur to anyone else, but for me it feels like time slows down, and I see every detail of the home. This may just be my imagination, but the house seems darker without Daisy there, like the shining sun has been sucked from the area, and only the dark shadow of what used to be a happy home remains.

This quick image is all it takes for me to break down entirely. I heave in air, but it doesn't seem to be enough for my lungs. I try to clear my thoughts, and focus on slowing down, but there are so many things swirling around in my head, and none of them are happy. Everything in my field of vision is blurry, and I close my eyes in an attempt to steady myself.

I can hear a voice calling out to me, but it is quiet and hard to reach from the state of panic I am in. I try to hone in on the voice, I can imagine it attempting to grab me, dragging me out of my head and back to reality. I focus all of my energy on listening, and I hear my name over and over again. *Abby! Abby! Abby are you alright? What's going on?*

Elias. It's Elias trying to help me. With a tremendous amount of effort, I manage to slow down my breathing, taking in deep gulps of air. *In and out, in and out.* Once I am back in my body, I feel Elias shaking me lightly. He's grabbing onto both of my shoulders, and is still saying my name urgently.

I slowly reopen my eyes, blinking a bit to adjust to the bright sunlight streaming into the car. It is only then, that I realize that we have come to a stop, and are no longer driving. He has pulled over on the side of the road, not far from where I started to lose it. In fact, I can still see Daisy's house behind us in the side view mirror, but I avert my gaze quickly. I do not want to have a mental breakdown.

Everything becomes much clearer now. I meet Elias's eyes, which are staring at me critically, examining my condition.

"Sorry," I whisper, ashamed that I couldn't hold it together just because of a stupid house.

He seems genuinely taken aback by this.

"Why on Earth would you be sorry? I'm just glad that you're okay, Abby," he sighs. "What happened back there? I mean, you don't have to share if you don't want to, but I would really appreciate it if you did. That really scared me."

I'm silent for a moment, debating whether or not I should tell him. Would he think I am crazy? No, of course not, because I'm not crazy. And even if I was, I know that Elias would never, ever judge me. Never.

"We just passed Daisy's house, and I haven't been there since," I stop, but he nods in understanding. "And I guess it just had an effect on me that I wasn't quite expecting."

"Oh my god, I'm so sorry. I had no idea. If I would've known-"

I cut his apology short. "No, you have nothing to be sorry for, it's not your fault. Do you think we could just not take this street next time?" I request.

He nods profusely. "Of course, absolutely." Then a little smile makes its way onto his face as he says, "I don't think I ever want to make you upset again."

The corners of my mouth turn upwards as well. "Sounds like a good plan to me!"

When I got home later that night I didn't mention any part of the situation from earlier to my family. I know, I know, I probably should tell them, but I honestly just couldn't bring myself to, afraid that they would worry and make a big deal out of it.

It is taco night in our household, and not long after I arrive back from physical therapy, Mom is already making dinner, so I sit at the kitchen island in order to keep her company.

"So, Abby, how was school today?" she inquires. She's on the other side of the counter, putting some shredded cheese into a large bowl for the four of us to share.

"Oh! It was pretty good overall. I didn't sleep much last night, so I'm a bit tired, but other than that, everything was fine," I reply, snatching the bag of cheese and eating some before handing it back to her.

"That's great, I'm glad you're able to enjoy school again," she comments, while shoving the shredded cheese back into the classic "cheese drawer" before closing the fridge.

My phone buzzes loudly on the granite countertop, causing me to pick it up and see what is going on.

It is, as usual, a text from Elias Smith.

Elias : Hey! Wanna discuss details for Friday?

"Who's that?" Mom asks, looking over her shoulder at me from the stove.

"It's Elias, can I hangout with him on Halloween?"

My mom smiles at me, clearly happy that I am making plans and not just moping around all night. "Of course! What are you guys going to do?" she responds, a little too eager, might I add.

"We don't know yet, that's exactly what he's texting me about right now. I'll let you know once we have something more solid, sound good?"

"Sounds great." She turned her back to me again, focusing on making our dinner.

Abigail : Sure! Any ideas?

Elias : Oh, geez. I don't really know?

Abigail : Well if you don't know how am I supposed to know?

Elias : Because you're smarter than me

Abigail : Sorry not sorry

Elias : :(

Abigail : OK, we're getting off topic

Elias : You're right

Elias: Idea: I can drive you straight from school over to my house, and we can just eat candy and watch horror movies

Abigail : But I don't like horror movies :(

Elias : OK, fine. MILDLY scary movies, I promise they won't
be too bad

Abigail : Fineeeeeeee

Elias : :)

He ends conversations like that often, and even though it
is just a smiley face through a phone, it totally feels like Elias. It's
such an Elias thing to do.

Turning off my phone, I explain the plan to my mom.

"That sounds like an awesome idea! Plus, that means that
I won't have to drive you anywhere," she winks. "It's a win-win
for me!"

"Oh, ha ha," I say, playfully sarcastic. "I-"

A loud bell rings, disrupting my next remark. It's the
dinner bell. She literally just rang the bell over my response.

Mom has a mischievous glint in her eyes, and her grin
says it all. I stick my tongue out at her, but don't have time for

much else as my tornado of a brother comes ripping through the kitchen.

"DINNER!!!" he screams, like some sort of 11th century viking has possessed the body of the eleven year old boy I see before me. He whips around the countertop, grabs a plate full of food, and starts eating before I can even start to get back into my wheelchair.

Mom rolls her eyes, but you can tell she's not really upset. She must be in a pretty good mood today, because usually she does not let that kind of behavior go unnoticed.

As my mom is helping me off of the barstool and back into my chair, Dad comes into the kitchen as well, although much more quietly than Alex, and scoops food onto his plate.

Once we are all sitting down at the table, Dad asks about our Halloween plans.

"Oh!" I exclaim, excited that I actually have something to say. "I'm going straight from school to Elias's house, and we're going to watch some movies together!" I share happily.

Both of my parents smile at each other, and it feels

private, like something I should not be watching. "That's great

honey!" Dad responds.

As soon as he's done with his sentence, Alex launches into

the whole story of what he is doing on Halloween. Something

about going trick or treating with a few members of his soccer

team. I am only half listening as I eat my dinner, and with a grin,

I think about how excited I am for Friday.

chapter 21:

As I roll out into the hallway after my fourth period class, the delighted conversations of students fill my ears. Locker doors slamming, loud chatting, some people are even yelling across the hall. This is the best time of day for almost everybody, lunch time. And today it is even better, because it is Friday, and also Halloween.

Spirits are high on my short journey to the courtyard. A lot of the student body is in costumes, with some being much more impressive than others, but that doesn't really matter now, does it?

When I got dressed this morning, I originally wasn't going to wear anything special, but my mom convinced me to at least put on a little something for Halloween. At the moment, I was wearing a white sweater and black jeans, along with some floppy Dalmatian ears on my head. It's as far as I could go without being too uncomfortable during school.

Rolling out into the courtyard, I see Elias sitting in our usual spot. When I saw him this morning, he was dressed as a pirate, wearing a white shirt with huge, billowing sleeves, an eyepatch, and a stuffed parrot duct taped, rather ungracefully, onto his shoulder. Now though, the parrot is sitting beside him on the bench and his eyepatch has been pushed back on top of his head. I guess I'm not the only one who has trouble staying comfortable in a costume throughout the entire school day.

As I settle myself next to him, I address the parrot first. "Good afternoon, Mr. Parrot, how are you doing today?"

Elias's mouth drops open and he gasps, playfully offended. "Abby! How dare you? For one, his name is Jimmy, not Mr. Parrot."

"I am so very sorry Jimmy, I had no idea. I won't get it wrong again, I promise." I stroke "Jimmy's" head, soothingly, to prove my point.

"And second of all, what about me??" he pouts.

I look back up at him. "What *about* you?"

"I would think that your best friend deserves a 'hello' but I guess I was wrong."

I giggle. "Hello Elias," I say, while patting his head like I did to the stuffed bird. "There, happy now?"

He nods. "Perfectly."

"So," he starts, after a few moments of silence while the two of us eat. "Excited for later?"

My smile grows, "I really am! Is it sad that I'm this excited to just watch movies and eat candy?"

"Absolutely not, I know it's probably not what you're used to, what with all of the partying you have done the last few years…"

I hit him on the arm, causing him to choke on his bite of food, before regaining his composure.

"But, what I was going to say, is that sometimes it can be just as fun to stay home and relax for the night," he finishes.

"Fine, I'll ignore the slight dig you took at me there, but I do agree with you on the last part."

"Awesome, so then we're on the same page. We are going to have the most fun out of everybody here tonight," he gestures towards the entire group of students in the courtyard. "And make all of these suckers wish they weren't invited to parties, like us! Deal?" He holds out his pinky finger for me to shake.

I wrap my finger around his, sealing in the pinky promise, "Deal!"

Elias's house is very similar to mine. Two stories and a basement, a large, bright kitchen opening up into a cozy living room, and the entire house has a very homey feel, just like mine does. I have never met Elias's mom or sister, but by looking around their home, I could tell that I would definitely like them, just based on how loving and together their space feels.

Elias told me that his dad would be out tonight, and his mom and his sister would be trick or treating, but not until a little bit later. As we move through the house, I wonder where they could be, not wanting to be caught off guard when I do finally meet them. From what I know about Elias's sister, I'm pretty sure that she is only a year younger than him, but she goes to some fancy art school thirty minutes away, which is why I have never met her before.

"My mom is picking Delilah up from school right now, but they should be back soon," Elias says, somehow reading my mind. "In the meantime, I thought that I could give you an exclusive tour of the house before we head downstairs to watch movies. How does that sound?" he suggests.

"Are you kidding, I would love a tour!" I laugh.

"Alright, m'lady! Then a tour you shall get!" And with that, he grabs onto the handlebars of my wheelchair and whirls me around in a circle before sprinting to the other side of the house.

I squeal loudly in surprise and keep on screaming until he comes to an abrupt stop right by the front door of the house.

"Elias!" I accuse, whipping my head back only to be met with him grinning, ear to ear. "You scared me! What was that for?"

"Eh, no reason really," he shrugs, a smile still plastered on his face. I scrunch my nose up at him and he does the same back before launching into a full on TED Talk about his home.

We walk through his dad's home office, their formal dining room, and a small bathroom before arriving back to the kitchen and living room, where we were before.

Just as Elias is explaining (in way too much detail) the kitchen remodeling his family had done two years ago, I hear the door to the mudroom open and shut.

Before I can even process what is happening, a girl with long raven hair and bright green eyes shoots through the doorway, looking around the room frantically, until her eyes lock onto me. She dashes over and immediately bends down to envelope me in a huge hug. Without a doubt, I know that this is Delilah.

She pulls away from me and I see that she and Elias share the same bright smile.

"Hi! I'm Delilah, Elias's sister. And you must be Abby! Right?" She introduces herself eagerly, and for some reason, she is clearly very excited to meet me.

"I am," I grin. "It's nice to finally meet you," I say enthusiastically.

"It's really nice to meet you too!" she gushes. "Elias talks about you non-stop…"

"Delilah!" Elias interrupts her. And I am secretly glad to see he is just as embarrassed as I was the first time my mom pulled that on me.

"Delilah! Stop bothering your brother and his friend!" A voice rings from the mudroom. Their mother walks into the open living room. She's almost an exact copy of Delilah, only slightly older, and with shining blue eyes, unlike the rest of the Smiths who have emerald green irises. She is shorter than both siblings, but she holds herself with so much grace, and power, that it's almost hard to tell.

"I wasn't *bothering* them, Mom! I was just saying hi," Delilah groans.

"Mhm sure, why don't you let me say hello now?"

"Alright," she sighs, and steps aside so that her mom can talk to me more easily.

"Abigail, I presume?" their mother asks, addressing me.

"Yes! Hello Mrs. Smith!" I say, reaching out my hand to shake hers. She smiles pleasantly and takes my hand, covering it with hers instead of shaking it.

"Oh, please. No need for such formalities, you can call me Julia."

"Alright then! Pleasure to meet you, Julia!"

"It is very nice to meet you as well, Abigail," she agrees, before letting my hand go and walking past me into the kitchen. She speaks to her son. "Hey, Elias?" Both of us turn in her direction.

"Yeah, Mom?"

"I'm assuming you want to finish Abigail's tour first…" Julia starts, before she is cut off.

"Wait, how did you know I was giving her a tour?" Elias interjects.

"Elias I'm your mother, I know you better than you know yourself," she answers, waving off the subject like it is no big deal. Elias still seems a little unsure, but he lets her continue. I quietly chuckle at his confusion.

"What I was trying to say was that after you are done showing Abigail around, I left a couple of big bags of candy for the two of you in the basement, and we have pizzas being delivered at six, if the two of you aren't stuffed with sweets by then."

"Awesome! Thanks, Mom!" Elias exclaims, giving his mother a quick hug and then jogging back over to me. "Are you ready to see upstairs, Abby?" he asks, not even waiting for an answer before starting to push me over to the staircase.

It is then that I remember my one problem. And it's a big one. "Um, actually Elias, I think it would be better if we just stayed on this floor," I say, apologetically.

He gives me an inquiring look. "Why? What's up?"

I look down into my lap. "It's just," I gesture down at my legs and the whole wheelchair thing.

He lets out an exasperated sigh. "Come on Abby! I've carried you before, it'll be perfectly fine, I promise!"

"Alright, alright!" I give in. And with that, Elias swiftly picks me up and carries me up the stairs like I weigh virtually nothing. He brings me into his bedroom and sets me on his bed before running back downstairs to get the wheelchair.

While he's gone, I take a short look around the room. It's a good size, bigger than my room but also not massive. He has a small closet with an open door that reveals the huge mess inside, a full size bed, which I must admit is very comfy, and a small desk in the corner of his room, near a window. Overall, the space is not very tidy, but also not crazy messy. There are a few things strewn on the floor, like a couple of clothing items and some books, but his bed is made, and his desk looks pretty neat.

As for the walls, he seems to have decorated them with stuff from all over the board. There are a couple of photos of him and his family taped up, as well as a few with some friends that I don't know. I also notice several of posters, most of them from Marvel movies, and some small drawings, which I guessed were done by him, pinned up here and there. It looks exactly like what I would expect from Elias, a little bit of everything.

He walks back through the door, wheelchair now in tow, and sets it by the bed so I can get up when I want to.

"So," he begins. "I guess we're starting this portion of the tour in my room." He reaches his arms out wide. "So, yeah, there's not much to see here." He starts listing the things in his room off one by one and points to them as he goes along. "There's my desk, my closet, my book shelf, and of course, my bed, which you are currently sitting on."

I giggle.

"Alright then, any questions so far?" he asks, like a true tour guide. He looks all around the room like there are more people than just me here, and when no one asks anything, he moves on. Wasting no time, Elias picks me up, puts me back into my chair, and leads me around the rest of the upper story.

When it is time to go back downstairs, Elias lifts me up again, and carries me all the way to the basement.

We pass his mom and sister, and I give them a little wave. They wave back, in addition to giving me warm smiles. They really have been very welcoming, and I am so grateful for that.

The basement looks absolutely amazing. It's like one of the ones you see in movies or television shows. Although it is just one open room, there is so much to do down here. There is a small bar, a pool table, a couple of old video game machines, and a comfy TV area, with a giant couch and stacks of movies surrounding the actual TV itself. I wheel myself over to the sitting area and before I can even try anything on my own, Elias lifts me up again and sets me back down gently onto one of the cushions. It is even softer and fluffier than it looks. Elias plops down next to me, and checks the time on his phone.

"It's already almost five," he states. I look at him quizzically, wondering what his point is. "Which means that we only have about an hour until the pizza comes, so we better get snacking on the candy now!"

He jumps back up and runs back to the bar, grabbing two huge bags of multicolored chocolates and candies.

"Elias!" I laugh. "Just because we can eat massive amounts of food tonight doesn't mean we necessarily should!" I trail him with my eyes, and I see the look of exaggerated shock that moves across his face. He stops in his tracks.

"Abby! That is precisely what it means! Come on, don't make me eat all of this candy alone," he begs. He gives me puppy eyes and holds the two bags of sweets up next to his face. "Please?"

"Fine! I give up on trying to stop us from getting a hundred cavities, you win!"

He runs gleefully back to the couch and jumps back onto it. "We're not going to get a hundred cavities, Bennett. You're always so dramatic," he jokes.

I think back to earlier this week at physical therapy. "I'm sorry, how am *I* the dramatic one?"

"You just are," he concludes, clearly not having any solid reasoning.

"Mhm sure, we can go with that," I mumble. Mimicking up my typical nose scrunch, he narrows his eyes at me before grabbing the remote and turning on the TV.

"So," he starts, recognizing that this is a debate he wouldn't win and changing the subject. "What do you want to watch?"

We end up watching a couple of older "horror" movies. By "horror" I mean very bad editing that makes the movies more funny than frightening. It worked out well, because I don't like scary movies, but Elias still wanted to watch something spooky in honor of Halloween. We also ate ALL of the candy and even some pizza, eating until we were sure we were about to pop.

Laying here in bed, I am still very full. Maybe that's the reason I can't sleep, or maybe it was all of the excitement of tonight. I had the absolute best time at the Smith's house, and I cannot wait to go back there soon.

But reliving the events of tonight over and over again in my head is not going to improve my sleeping problem. I've been trying to fall asleep for hours now with no luck. It is already the early hours of the morning. At least tomorrow (or would it be today?) is Saturday, so I can sleep in as late as I want.

In an attempt to slow down my mind, I decide to mindlessly scroll through my different social media apps, starting with Instagram.

But of course, this is no help. Actually, it makes things even worse.

The problem is, I still follow my old friend group on Instagram, so my entire feed is full of pictures and videos from the various parties going on tonight.

Overall I don't care too much about the partying. Did I used to like going to them? Well, yes. But would I even want to be seen at one now? Probably not. So I don't really mind that I wasn't invited.

The real thing that bothers me are the pictures of what used to be my close friends. According to Natalie's posts, they all coordinated their costumes, each was a different social media app. I think back to the time when I was a part of that group. Every year we would dress up together in costumes of Natalie's choice, but I never really minded. I was just happy to be included. And although I know I should not care, considering the wonderful time I had with Elias, it still hurts to know that I am not part of that group anymore.

A few stray tears fall down my cheeks as I reminisce on all of my previous Halloweens. Even when we were in Elementary school and we didn't go to parties, Natalie and I still had our little group that we would lead trick-or-treating around the neighborhood and stuff our faces with candy until our parents told us it was time for bed.

This is the first year that I can remember that I haven't spent the entire night with Natalie and the mixed members of our little clique.

It pains me that although Natalie is in the same boat, she doesn't seem to care that I am gone. All she cares about is her popularity, and by the looks of it, she's got plenty of that.

There are two new girls in the photos that I don't recognize. Most of the other people I know from spending time with them when I was a part of the group. But these two people I had never met before.

The realization hits me like a dagger through the heart. These girls are Daisy's and I's replacements. When two girls leave, two more are allowed in. Natalie's logic makes sense on a catty high school level, but on a more human level, I cannot believe her.

Replacing me is one thing. Natalie does not want to be my friend anymore and she has made that entirely clear.

But replacing Daisy? That is absolutely heartless. Daisy died. Daisy did not betray Natalie in any way. She did not choose her fate, and trying to put another person in her place feels disrespectful to her memory.

Anger fills all of my senses. It's just not fair. How dare she be so nonchalant about this entire thing? You cannot just erase someone's entire life, their entire existence, because you want another little minion to control.

I close out the Instagram app quickly in an attempt to stop myself from getting too furious.

I think about calling Natalie. Finally standing up to her and screaming at her through the phone. But chances are, she wouldn't answer. Not only because it is so late, but also because I'm sure she still has my number, and she most definitely does not want to talk to me. I could leave a voicemail though. Then at least I can feel like I am doing something.

My finger is hovering over the call button, and I am about to press it, but something in my heart stops me. A single thought makes its way to the forefront of my brain.

What would Elias think?

I ponder it for a moment, my rage slowly dissipating. He would tell me to keep calm, and not do anything I might regret. He would say that I should get back at her in time, and the best way to do that is to show her that she has no control over me anymore. That I don't need her, and I can accomplish anything I put my mind to.

Elias is right, yelling at Natalie wouldn't solve anything. So, I put the phone back down on my nightstand, turning it off in the process, and lie back down on my bed, tightly shutting my eyes.

chapter 22:

The elevator doors open, and Mom and I move down the familiar hallways of the medical center, stopping outside of Dr. Smith's office. Although I have been back here a few times since he told me I would be able to walk again, I haven't gotten any X-rays in a while. And although they are expected to go well, Dr. Smith wanted to check to make sure nothing is going wrong, and I am still on track to be walking before the end of the school year.

As we walk up to the front desk, and Mom checks me in, I think about how familiar this office has become. Honestly, I've been here so many times in the past year that this place doesn't scare me anymore. Usually when I'm with Dr. Smith I get good news, so I feel, well, almost joyful whenever I'm here now.

We sit in a small waiting room for a little bit, but there is no one else here so we get called back pretty quickly.

A young woman with a kind smile calls my name and my mom and I walk through the waiting area and back to one of the

225

rooms with an examination table and other materials that you would typically see in a doctor's office.

After we are led into the room, another woman, who looks older than the first and is wearing a lab coat, brings me back to get my legs x-rayed. I'm used to the experience by now, so the dark room and the big machines aren't nearly as threatening as they were a few months ago.

I stay as still as possible, and soon I'm returning to the examination room, where my Mom is waiting patiently.

I'm assuming that Dr. Smith isn't very busy, because almost as soon as the technician shuts the door, it pops right back open, and in walks Dr. Smith, as peppy as always.

"Hello Ms. Abigail!" he greets as he comes through the doorway. "And Mrs. Bennett! Always a pleasure to see you both!" He seems very happy and cheerful, which boosts my mood.

"Hello Dr. Smith!" I smile, matching his excitement. I find myself thinking back to all of the times that Elias has evoked the same response from me. I guess the Smith family just has that effect on people

My mom is less enthusiastic, and settles for a polite smile at the doctor, before returning to her usual neutral face. Mom has never liked this doctor's office, I think it pains her to be here in the first place, given the way everything happened.

He doesn't seem to care about her apparent coldness, I'm assuming either because he's used to it or he understands how she's feeling. Either way, he moves on quickly, pinning the black and white x-ray pictures up on a white board. He flips a switch on the wall, and the entire board is flooded with light, making it easy to see the photos and the different bones in my legs.

"So, Abby, you are looking perfect!" he says, grinning.

"Really?" I question, a little hesitant to accept that nothing has gone wrong.

"Really! The physical therapy you are doing has not negatively affected your legs in any way, and they are still healing up as expected! That being said, my original timeline still applies.

Although you are getting better, you're still going to have to wait a few months before you're back on your feet again," he explains. That's alright though, I wasn't expecting to be able to walk anytime soon. In fact, these results are even better than what I had prepared for!

"Thank you so much Dr. Smith!" I exclaim happily, showing him that I am not at all disappointed by the fact that I still have work to do.

"Yes, thank you so much," my mom beams, much more relaxed now that she knows nothing is wrong.

He flashes us a grateful smile before explaining he has other patients to see and telling us to book a follow up appointment.

We walk back to the car and load up the wheelchair. When Mom climbs into the driver's seat, she turns to me before she backs out of the parking space.

"I have an idea," she starts.

I am immediately intrigued. "And what would your idea be?" I inquire.

She looks me right in the eyes, and I can see mischief gleaming in hers. "He said you should be ready to walk in a few months, right?"

"That is correct, yes."

"And prom is in April?"

I had already assumed that I would not be going to prom, so I didn't know the exact date, but I knew it was in the springtime. I nod in response, still curious about where this is going.

"We're going to get you walking by prom." She says it like it's obvious. I must look skeptical because she speaks again, adding on to her previous remark. "Safely, of course, and we'll get Dr. Smith's permission, but if you work hard, I think we can do it."

I grin, "That would be amazing! But I'm assuming that's not all there is to your grand idea?"

She flashes a smile and I can see the excitement filling her expressions. "I think we should make it a surprise."

I can tell that she is trying to gauge my reaction as her eyes search my face for an answer on whether or not I like this plan.

Naturally, I love it.

"Are you sure you want to try to speed things up, Abigail? It's going to be hard, and you don't want to rush a process as important as this one," Sam warns.

I had just told her and Lili about my new goal, to be walking in time for Junior prom.

I had made Mom call Dr. Smith right after she had suggested the new timeline, since I was concerned about the same things that Sam was.

The doctor said that he believed I would be fine, and he honestly thought that I had nothing to worry about. After all, it was only about a month earlier than expected, and although it would require more commitment on my part, it should work out well.

So far, I have kept my new objective a relatively closely guarded secret. I mean, I have told the rest of my family and my physical therapists, of course, but I haven't told any of my friends or classmates. Not even Elias. He was the one I wanted to surprise the most.

When I told Sam and Lili, I made sure that I got to speak to them alone, while Elias was busy organizing the exercise equipment. I made it very clear that neither of them should mention any of this to him, as I wanted it to remain a surprise.

With the excitement of the future looming over me, I was now even more determined to get this right.

"I'll be fine, Dr. Smith approved it, and I really, really want to do this," I insist to Sam.

Her and Lili share a look, as if they are making sure they are both on the same page.

After what feels like forever, they both turn back to me.

"Let's do this!' Lili bubbles.

Just then Elias appears behind Lili's shoulder.

"Let's do what?" he wonders. Oh shoot, he heard us. The three of us share a look of slight panic, before Lili saves us.

"Oh! We were just talking about how Abby is starting on some new ankle exercises today," Lili replies, smiling at me.

I'm guessing that this statement isn't exactly false, which is why she is able to come up with it on the spot so quickly.

Elias looks a little bit confused about why we're so excited about some new simple ankle movements, but he grins at me regardless, and looks just as thrilled for me as Lili does.

He's so sweet, which makes me feel worse for keeping something from him, but I remind myself that this won't last forever, and he will be over the moon when I surprise him in just a few short months.

True to Lili's word, we mostly work on my ankles during my session. I wiggle them around and turn them in circles, and we practice a few new things that I am tasked to do at home, twice a day.

When we are done, I ride home with Elias, as usual, and we talk about school and all the homework we have to do tonight. Both of us have a lot of calculus work, and we complain about it for a while, until we pull up to my driveway.

One of my parents is usually home when I get back, but Elias has become accustomed to walking me up to my garage door and opening it for me before he drives back home.

As I wheel away from him and towards the door to my house I make sure to turn around and wave at him as he drives away.

He has his windows down today, so I take this opportunity to yell "See you tomorrow!" at him.

"See ya Bennett!" he calls back at me. I try to scrunch my nose up at him, in disapproval of the name, but he's gone before I even get the chance.

Tuesday morning I arrive at our joint desk in calculus before Elias, which rarely happens. He is usually here much earlier than I am, but I guess today is the exception.

I wait for him for a while, wondering where he is as the minutes tick by, getting closer and closer to seven thirty, when the first period starts.

The bell signaling the start of the day rings throughout the entire school, and a certain boy is still not here.

I pull out my phone and get ready to text him, worried that Elias is sick or hurt in some way.

Mr. Carson immediately instructs us to take out our notebooks and start on the warm up, but because I sit at the back of the classroom, I can get away with sending a quick message.

Where are you?

I type, but before I can hit send, a commotion happens at the front of the classroom, drawing my eyes up from the screen.

Elias stands by the whiteboard, the wide open door still swinging behind him, looking disheveled and sweaty.

Everyone in room 211 stares at him, looking for any excuse to not be working out a long math problem.

Elias looks down, embarrassed. He was clearly trying to get here on time, and was just a little bit too slow.

"Sorry I'm late, Mr. Carson. It won't happen again, I promise," he mutters to the teacher. He still has his head lowered so it's hard to hear, but seeing as the classroom has gone dead silent, I can still make out what he is saying.

He quickly shuffles down the middle aisle to the back of the room, where I am sitting waiting for him. As soon as he sits down, the chatter in the classroom picks back up again, and it isn't nearly as awkward.

Elias takes all of his materials out and sets them on the desk before he even acknowledges me.

However, when he does, he acts like nothing has happened. The only trace of the situation that just occurred is the pink tint on Elias' cheeks and a few stray drops of sweat that are no doubt there from rushing to get to school on time. But other than that, he still puts on his ear to ear smile, and seems to be in a much peppier mood than that of a few minutes ago.

"Good morning Bennett! And how might you be on this lovely autumn day?"

Wondering what possibly could have happened to him this morning, I raise my eyebrows at him as if to say *what on Earth happened to you?*

He understands my gesture and immediately launches into a recap of his day so far.

"Delilah needed the car today, which usually would be fine, but she only just told me this morning so I didn't wake up early enough to get on the correct bus which meant that I had to take a later one, but this bus didn't drop off at the normal stop. Instead, it spit me out about five blocks from the school, and I was already late, might I add, so I had to run to get here," he rambles. "Honestly it's a miracle I got here when I did!" he adds.

Once I am sure he is done with his story and I deem it safe to react, I give him a sympathetic look. "Oh no, that really sucks, I'm sorry."

He seems to appreciate my contribution and nods aggressively in response. "I know right?"

A switch flips in Elias and all of a sudden he seems to have forgotten about his troubles, as he shifts his focus to me.

"Anyway, enough about me, how's your day going, Abby?"

I'm not gonna lie, this stumps me a little bit. And not even the question itself, but this boy's willingness to move onto my feelings just like that. Anyone else I know would go on for the entire day about how horrible their morning was, but Elias seems to just brush it off. He's so positive, it amazes me every time. I'm not a pessimist, but even I am never as fully happy as Elias effortlessly is.

I don't realize that I have zoned out until the boy waves his hand in front of my face.

"Hello? Earth to Abby," he jokes.

I quickly shake my head as a way to fling off the remaining daze I was in. However, I am still bewildered by the person in front of me.

"I'm sorry, I'm good, but are you really okay? Just like that?" His expression is now one of confusion. He has one eyebrow cocked up and he's looking at me like I'm crazy. I continue to explain, "Because you know, I'm fine if you want to keep complaining, you had a pretty crappy start to the day and I would understand if-"

He finally interjects, "Abby I'm okay, I promise you, I just don't feel like it's that big of a deal. Sure, I had a rough start, so what? I'm not going to let it ruin a perfectly good day." His tone is incredulous, like he doesn't understand that he is unlike most people, or at least the ones that I know.

He widens his smile even further, trying to convince me that he's okay and I give in, beaming back at him.

"Okay then, Mr. Positivity. Want to work on the warm-up?" I request, only to be met with a deep groan from Elias.

"Do we have to, Abby? Even Mr. Positivity can't be positive about calculus, don't make me do it, please!" he begs dramatically, falling over into my lap.

I push him back into an upright position, and insist that we've got to get started.

"Alright, alright, but I can't promise that I won't protest it the entire time," he mutters, clearly upset that I am forcing him to actually do the classwork.

Aha, so it turns out his weakness is math, then. But I suppose that no one can really be happy when learning about integrals and derivatives, can they?

The second hand on the clock at the front of the classroom *ticks ticks ticks*. All thirty of us students stare intently at it, waiting for the minute hand to move forward one place, letting us leave for our forty five minutes to eat and escape from school work. My history teacher is still droning on and on about our homework for the night, but that information will probably be online later, so no one is really paying attention.

Tick, tick, tick, tick. The suspense is killing me, I just want to get out of here. I'm hungry, and I'm tired, and I'm burnt out, and it's only half way through the day.

Tick, tick, tick, tick. Come on, come on, please hurry up, I don't know how much longer I can stand this lecture.

Riiinnggggg! Finally. Lunch time!

As soon as we are released, everyone in the room is talking loudly, and running out of the class as fast as they can.

The teacher tries to get one last sentence in, but she is drowning in a sea of teenagers, and I see her give up and plop back down at her desk.

I am one of the last ones to leave, because I don't want to be trampled, but I still make my way into the hallway quickly, and push myself forward towards the doors to the courtyard.

Of course, I have to sneak by Natalie's locker to get there, which is no small feat when it's pretty easy to spot me in my wheelchair. Let's just hope she's indifferent towards me today.

I pass by this area everyday on my way to Elias. Most days, she either ignores me or simply laughs behind my back, but today she has her eyes on me before I am even near her. She is watching me with that chilling sneer on her face. A look that reminds me just how far beneath her I am, both metaphorically and physically.

As I get closer and closer she doesn't make any move to approach me, just continues glaring at me condescendingly.

I am almost next to her, when I have a brief memory of when we were much younger.

In my head, we were only eleven, and it was our first day of middle school together.

I remember it being so, so early. The first day back from summer break was never easy, but it was so much worse when you had to start at a new school.

I was tired, but I was also wired with nerves and excitement, so I ended up being very jittery, and I was playing with the zipper of my jacket.

Up and down. Up and down.

It was an unusually cool day for August because it had rained the night before, but I couldn't be bothered by the cold.

I was a middle schooler now, middle schoolers were brave, they aren't ever cold.

I felt so old and so mature, even though I was barely double digits.

"Abby, Natalie! Stand in front of the school for a picture!" My mom called out. She had driven us to school that morning, as Natalie's mom was busy at work.

"No, a little to the left girls! Come towards me a bit! Yes! There you go, now smile!"

Natalie and I posed, arms around each other, flashing toothy grins full of gaps that would eventually be pulled together by braces. Bunched in our hands were our new schedules, which we had already compared to see what classes we had together. It was going to be so weird not seeing each other all day.

Mom lowered her phone, done taking photos, and seemed to take a moment to smile at us, a far off look on her face that suggested she was reminiscing on all of the times that had led up to this moment.

We still had a few moments before we had to go inside, and now that the start time was closing in, I was progressively feeling more and more nervous. This school was so much bigger than my old one, and what if Natalie and I never got to see each other? She was my best friend, and though I didn't want to admit it, I was scared to let elementary school go.

I must've looked worried, because Natalie gripped tightly onto my hand, and squeezed so that I would look over at her.

When I did, her face was calm. She said to me, "It's okay, Abby, I know that this is a little bit scary, but we will get through this together, okay?"

I nodded at her to show I understood, feeling a little bit better already.

As if reading my thoughts she added, "And we will always be best friends, I promise."

This made me smile and I told her that she would always be my best friend too. For ever and ever.

The five-minute bell rang, and my mom gave me one last hug before nudging us towards the doors to our new school.

And together, Natalie and I walked in, hand in hand, ready to face the world.

The present-day world is not nearly as pleasant. I manage to pull myself together and get past Natalie and her snickering clique.

However, once I am out of her line of vision, and I no longer feel her eyes stabbing the back of my head, I let myself shed a tear. Not for Natalie herself, but for the people we once were.

chapter 23:

When I pop open my eyes on Wednesday morning, I can already hear commotion happening downstairs, telling me that Alex has gotten up early today.

He and my mom are arguing about something, and from what I can hear, I'm guessing it's about some sort of candy? My bet would be that he wants to take something to school in his lunch that my mother does not approve of.

I text her to let her know that I need help getting ready, and brace for the storm about to make its way into my room.

Of course, Alex follows my Mom and continues the argument into my bedroom, so I have to listen to it while I get ready.

"Mom, please! All of the other kids take treats in their lunch! I'm not lying, I promise!" he begs.

"Alex!" she shouts, tersely. She moves around my room, grabbing clothes for me that I point out while still continuing to fight back. "I am NOT letting you take a full size box of candy to school with you! What kind of mother would I be if I allowed that to happen?"

I don't mean to, but I accidentally let out a chuckle at this sentence, just because of how preposterous Alex's request is. Why on Earth does he think taking an entire box of candy for lunch is a good idea. Clearly he is already hyper enough without the sugar.

When I make a noise, Alex turns to me, like he hadn't noticed I was there and cheers a bright "Hi, Abby!" before launching back into full pouty mode. He looks at Mom, making his eyes big and round and puffing out his bottom lip.

This usually works on her, but not today.

"You are not bringing that candy to school Alex, sorry. End of discussion," she declares definitively.

Alex puts on a full frowny face before stomping out of my room and pounding back downstairs.

My mother rolls her eyes to me. "That kid, my goodness," she sighs, exasperated, before helping me into the bathroom to change and brush my teeth.

She waits outside the door until I'm ready, not caring enough to go back downstairs only for a few minutes, and then helps me down to the kitchen.

There, we find Alex, staring sadly into a box of M&Ms. He has opened it, clearly meaning to eat them while Mom was helping me, so that he could at least get a taste of sugar before school, but he is not currently chewing on any. He looks down into the box gloomily, and I can't help but wonder what the heck is wrong with him.

Mom's face turns soft, and she seems to decide to be sweet about whatever is going on here. She walks over to him slowly, and places her hand on his shoulder.

"Alex, what's wrong, baby?" she asks gently.

"Look," he states miserably. "The box is barely even full, and I haven't eaten any yet, this is just how it came!" he cries, like some major offense has been committed against him.

Almost all of my mother's sympathy vanishes. "That's what you're upset about? Goodness, Alex, I thought that I had made you sad! But, no, if this is just about a box of candy, I am not having it!"

She takes the box of M&Ms and tosses it back into the cupboard. She turns away from the door, getting ready to close it, but then pauses and sighs. She quickly picks up two Hershey's Kisses from inside and throws them into Alex's lunchbox.

"Now get ready for school, or else you'll be late," she advises.

Alex agrees, grinning from ear to ear in glee, a new pep in his step.

Mom gives me a look that says, *Can you believe this kid?*

And I give her a shrug back that suggests *He's a middle school boy, what do you expect?*

"Good morning, class!"

Silence.

"Alrighty, well, today we will be starting on a group project!"

A collective groan.

"But because I am such a nice teacher, you get to pick your partners!"

A loud cheer and a few thank yous.

"See, I knew you guys would like that. Just please, please, please pick a person you think you'll work well with. And try to work with someone new, make another friend in the process!"

Nobody is going to listen to that advice, that's for sure, and it seems like Mr. Carson knows this because he doesn't work too hard to stop everybody from making that specific face across the room to their friends, and shouting out names.

Luckily, I don't have to look too far to meet Elias's eyes and nod, agreeing that we will, obviously, be working together.

Mr. Carson yells over the class to get our attention again, before further explaining the guidelines of the assignment.

We are supposed to find a container of some sort, it can be any product, but it needs to be something with extra material that we feel can be decreased. We need to use optimization to figure out the dimensions of the new container that uses less materials but still fits the same amount of product inside.

It sounds confusing, but I don't think even the easiest calculus project that Mr. Carson could have come up with would make complete sense to me. At least we get to do it with another person.

The teacher lets us know that it is due next Monday, so we have about five days to work on it, which means we have to get started soon.

Luckily, Mr. Carson is giving us class time today to start planning with our partners, so we can begin working on it right away.

As soon as he lets us go, I turn to Elias, only to find he is already looking at me, waiting to begin our project.

"Let's brainstorm some ideas, Abby. What are your first thoughts?" he questions, taking out a piece of paper to jot down notes.

I make a show of tapping my head, to let Elias know that I am thinking about it.

Hmmmm. Some sort of product that is in a wasteful container? That's when a bright idea pops into my head. *That's it! The candy box this morning!*

"Elias!" I exclaim, excited about my thought.

He looks up from his note page, where he had apparently begun doodling, and smiles. I think he is able to tell that I have a plan in mind.

"This morning, before school, my little brother was complaining about an M&Ms box, because there was barely any candy inside, and the packaging suggested way more product than there actually was. Do you think that would work for our project?" I inquire.

He seems to like my proposition. "Yeah, actually I think that would! I've totally experienced that before! Great job, Abby!" he congratulates, writing *M&Ms box - too small!* onto his scrap of notebook paper.

"Want to go to my house later to work on it? After your physical therapy session?" he requests.

"Sure, sounds good!" I reply.

The rest of the day passes me by, and with every new minute I grow more and more giddy for tonight. I don't even care that I'm only going to Elias's to work on a school project, I'm still excited to hang out with him. I am also secretly hoping to see his sister again, so that I can get to know her a little bit better.

When I arrived at Elias's house earlier, no one other than the two of us were there, and that is still the way it remains now.

We are sitting on the floor of Elias's room, which is luckily carpeted, and I am leaning against his closet door to help stabilize myself. Elias is perched directly across from me, examining some of the papers that are scattered on the ground between us. They lie on the soft floor, along with two pencils, a calculator, and a box of M&Ms that has mostly been eaten.

We have completed most of our calculations for the project, and now it comes down to creating a prototype of our product and making a presentation on everything we have come up with. Both of these things we planned to split up and do separately this weekend, that way we don't have to worry about finding another time to meet up.

Elias seems to be checking our math for the hundredth time, but I might as well let him. He makes a few humming sounds here and there, but does not move to change anything, so I'm assuming it is all correct.

As he does this, I take a closer look around the walls of his bedroom. I focus on the few pictures of himself he has by his bed, pondering them more in depth than I did on Halloween.

One photo in particular catches my eye. It's of Elias and three other people, who I now know to be the rest of the Smiths. They are all on a snowy mountain somewhere, wearing snow pants and puffy jackets. Each person is proudly brandishing a pair of skis, holding them up in front of their bodies.

It's hard to tell with their bulky helmets and other gear on, but Elias looks to be a couple of years younger than he is now.

I have never really been a huge winter sports fan, but I've gone skiing with my family a few times over the years. I did stop a while ago though, so my current situation has not really changed anything in that regard.

"Do you still ski?" I ask Elias, out of the blue. He glances up from our work to address me, but looks confused as to why I am asking in the first place. I think I notice a wave of panic flick across his face, and I faintly wonder what that is about.

"The picture on your wall," I clarify, pointing to the glossy photo I was gazing at.

His shoulders slump a little bit, and he takes a while to answer, as if he is contemplating what he wants to say. I secretly hope that he shares with me whatever is bothering him, but it's clearly a touchy subject.

After what feels like forever, Elias finally answers my question. "I used to, but I don't anymore," he says cautiously, like he is choosing his words carefully.

"Is there a reason why you stopped?" I question delicately.

It is rare that Elias seems distant and hurt, but in this moment, he does. I can't pinpoint exactly what has happened, but the work he was looking at lies discarded on the carpet, and his usual smile is not anywhere to be found. His eyes are glassy, and I realize that I've clearly touched a nerve.

I quickly backtrack, trying to get the mood back to fun and playful like it was before. "I'm so so sorry, you don't have to tell me if you don't want to. I promise I won't be offended, and I don't want you to feel pressured at all," I rush.

He holds his hand up, and his eyes look guiltily into mine. "No, no please don't apologize," he pleads. "I want to tell you, I promise, it's just-" he pauses. "It's just difficult," he finishes.

I hold his gaze, and nod in understanding. "Take all of the time you need, and I mean that." I really, really do. I don't know what he is about to share, or what painful memories are plaguing him, but I do know that whatever it is, it is important to Elias. Something he holds as a part of his identity.

He takes a few deep breaths to steady himself. *In and out, in and out, in and out.*

When he speaks again, it comes out of nowhere, and it startles me how quiet he is. Elias is usually so loud and boisterous, but right now he is meek and timid, a new side to his personality that I have not witnessed yet.

"That picture was taken when I was 13 years old," he whispers, doing a small gesture up to the now significant photo on the wall. "It was actually one of the last times I went skiing. My family still goes up to the mountains every so often, but always just to see the scenery.

"A few weeks after that photo, my family and I went to Steamboat, where we usually skiied. We rented a condo, towed up our skis and poles, you know, the type of thing we had done a thousand times." He stops again here, placing his right hand on his chest, inhaling slowly a few more times before meeting my eyes again. I nod at him, encouraging him to go on.

"My parents were hungry and tired, and they asked Delilah and I if we wanted to go get lunch, but it was such a nice day, and we didn't want to get off of the slopes yet. They decided that because I was thirteen and Delilah was twelve, we could ski one more run alone, as long as we promised to go straight to the lounge afterward. Delilah and I, of course, agreed, so Mom and Dad went into the restaurant, and Delilah and I rode the chairlift up to the top of the mountain.

"Dad had told us to make sure we were careful, and instructed us to only go down a blue or green run, as this was what we were accustomed to. Delilah wanted to try a harder trail, but I insisted we just ski down one of the green ones we were familiar with." He starts to choke up here, and his voice becomes strained. I notice tears rising up in his eyes, and I feel so sympathetic for the boy in front of me. I don't even have the whole story yet, but I can just imagine a little thirteen year old Elias and his sister, so gleeful to be skiing without their parents, feeling so proud and so mature. All those emotions that were clearly going to be wiped away in only a short moment.

"I'm still not quite sure exactly how it happened, but, we think a snowboarder clipped one of her skis from behind and then the next thing I saw was Deliah barreling at full speed towards the trees on the side of the run. I tried to stop her. Tried using all the skills I had learned in my lessons to chase after her and try to help, but it was too late. She hit a tree as the idiot snowboarder took off at full speed down the mountain. We never saw him again."

"The next thing I knew, Delilah was on her back in the snow. My head hovered over hers, and I searched her face, asking over and over again if she was okay. She told me yes, and at first I thought she was. But then she tried to get up, and, Abby, that's where everything went wrong." Silent tears are now fully streaming down Elias's face, and my eyes are threatening to spill over too.

"She couldn't move her legs Abby, no matter how hard she tried. She-" At this point I can't stand it anymore. I lean across the space between us, as far as I can, and pull Elias deep into my chest, tugging him closer and closer to me. He buries his face into my shoulder, and I can feel his tears seeping through the thin fabric of my shirt onto my skin. I honestly couldn't care less. I am crying onto his clothes as well, so why would I mind at all.

We embrace for a long time. It could've been minutes, it could've been hours, but I didn't care, I know that he needed it. We both needed it. So we stayed together for a while.

When we eventually pull apart, his face is red and puffy from weeping, and I'm positive that I look one hundred times worse than him.

"It's so hard to see someone you love in so much pain," he continues. He gives me a weak smile, and chuckles a little bit. "So, I know what you're going through right now. I've been through a very similar experience with my sister."

"Hmm, yeah I guess you do. It sucks doesn't it?" I let out a small laugh at this statement, and the coincidence that we met and both have experience with the same thing.

His smile grows wider, "Yeah it really does suck," he assures. "But, it does get better Abby, I promise. She did all of the physical therapy, put in all of the work, and look at her now! You saw how joyful and full of life she is! You'll be there someday too, I know it," he states with confidence. Besides his still swollen face,

Elias is nearly back to his normal, radiant self, and that energy is transferring over to me.

Everything makes so much more sense now. The way he is so understanding of my situation, the time he spends working at the physical therapy center, his ease with my wheelchair, everything. I mean, no wonder he is so good at helping me in and out of the car, he must've helped his sister do it a thousand times.

I beam at him, a new wave of motivation coursing through my veins. "Thank you Elias, so much."

He tilts his head to the side. "For what?"

"For telling me your story, for sharing such a personal experience with me, for helping me through all of this. Just thank you," I explain.

"There's no need to thank me for all of that Abby, I'm just being a decent person!" he retaliates, but I can tell that deep down he appreciates the comment, recognizing all of his efforts.

chapter 24:

The bright yellow sun shines down on the school courtyard, effectively cancelling out the cool autumn air, so when you are in the sun, it's a fairly nice fall day.

Elias and I had purposely made an effort to sit in the path of the sun today, as we knew that the shade would be way too chilly, and then we would spend the entirety of our lunch break shivering and miserable. I look over to the few poor unfortunate kids who arrived late to lunch and are sitting in the shade of the building at the moment. They look absolutely freezing. Seems like Elias and I made the right decision to move.

There is a flat piece of tinfoil in my lap, on which lies a peanut butter and jelly sandwich on wheat bread, my favorite.

"So, Abby," Elias begins, and I whip my head around so I am directly looking at him again, instead of across the courtyard.

"Yes, Elias?"

"Tell me something about yourself that I don't already know," he prompts.

I playfully narrow my eyes at him. "And why would I do that?"

"Because we have nothing else to talk about," he whines.

I still am not convinced.

He gives in. "Fine, fine, I have to play as well. So you tell me something about you, and I'll tell you something about me. Sound good?"

I grin, "Yep! Sounds great!"

I think for a second about what I should say. We've already discussed the surface level things, I mean we talk every day, so I'm going to have to look deep into my mind to find something we haven't discussed yet.

It doesn't take long until an idea pops into my head. "Okay, I've got something," I proclaim.

Elias stares eagerly at me, waiting for me to say more.

"When I was a little kid, I used to make these vlog type videos on my Mom's computer. I called them 'The Abby Show,' and they can still be found on her laptop to this day."

This clearly intrigues him, as he is grinning from ear to ear. "Oh boy, Abby, I seriously cannot wait to see those!"

"Well, that's too bad because you will never see them!" I jest.

"Nope, I will find a way to watch them somehow," he vows, determined. "I may even break into your house to steal your mom's computer."

"I wouldn't do that if I were you, my dad would kick your ass, he knows karate you know," I counter.

"Well then, Abby, I guess I'll just have to fight your dad!" he brags, throwing a few punches into the air.

This sends me into a fit of laughter, and by the time I am pulled out of it, I am anxious to learn Elias's fun fact.

"Okay, I went, now it's your turn!" I maintain.

But as Elias opens his mouth to speak, the bell on the side of the school rings out loudly, and just like that, our lunch break is over. I audibly scoff and cross my arms over my chest.

"Oops, sorry Bennett, but you will not be learning anything new about me today!" Elias chuckles, clearly amused. Before I can protest or demand justice, Elias waves and jogs back into the building, already heading back to class.

That was so unfair! I grumble as I pick up my trash and head back into the corridors as well. I'll get him back tomorrow, I'll make sure he goes first.

The next morning I awake to a new text from Elias on my phone screen. However, while my mood initially lifts, it soon deflates when I read the content of the message.

Elias : Abby, I'm so sorry but I feel really really sick today, so I won't be at school :(I just wanted to let you know.

Abby: Oh no! Are you alright?

Elias: I'm fine :) I should be back at school by Monday, don't worry.

Great, now I'm going to have to try to navigate the entire school day without Elias. I sit next to him in nearly all of my classes, and at lunch, so I'm going to be pretty lonely today.

My day is not off to the best start, and it gets even worse when I get to school and sit down at my empty desk in calculus.

When I turn to face the front of the classroom, there is an announcement written up on the board.

We will be doing partner worksheets today. Please try to find a person and sit next to them before our class begins.

Shoot. Now I have to find a new person in the class. Someone to work with all day today. This is a major problem; I have only ever talked to Elias in this class, and I haven't made too many other friends since my accident.

My eyes dart around the room as I look for someone who is sitting alone like me; someone without a partner yet.

To my dismay, most of the students seem to be paired up already, chatting animatedly with each other. But one girl sits in the front corner of the room, all by herself. She's caught my eye before, because of the bright purple pixie cut she sports, but I don't know her name or anything else about her.

Her brown eyes are frantically searching the room, the same as mine, and it's not long before our gazes meet. She beams at me, an unspoken understanding being conveyed through our expressions. Looks like I have found my new partner.

The girl gathers all of her belongings and strolls across the room to my desk.

When she reaches me, she sets her stuff down and introduces herself.

"Hi there! My name is Claire," she greets kindly.

"I'm Abigail, but you can call me Abby," I smile warmly.

She sits herself down in Elias's usual seat, and while she does this, I find myself staring at her lavender hair. It's so daring, so outgoing, that for a second I find myself wishing I could rock that same hairstyle. I could never dye my hair such a vibrant color though, I don't think it would suit me.

She is dressed casually in an oversized hoodie with leggings and wears large, round glasses that suit her face perfectly.

To be honest, I could probably use some more friends at school anyway, and this might be the perfect opportunity. After all, I can't only hang out with Elias forever, I need more people to be with if he is absent, like today.

"Alright then Abby, how are you today?" she asks, looking back at me instead of her notebooks.

I think about my answer for a moment, deciding whether to give my usual "good" as a cop out answer, or explain how I wasn't really having the best day so far.

In an attempt to make a greater bond with Claire, I decide to go with the truth. "Actually, I'm not doing too great, but overall I'm fine. Happier now that I've found a partner, what about you?"

"Me too! Geez, finding partners or groups in classes when you don't know too many people is so stressful!" she agrees.

"Right? It's like teachers don't understand how difficult it is when you have to try to talk to new people in school."

"Yes! Exactly! It's scary, man. You seem nice though so I'm glad we get to work together today!"

"Thank you! I'm happy we get to work together too! This could be kind of fun," I suggest, but almost immediately take it back. "Or, as fun as completing math problems can be."

"Definitely," she laughs.

I end up having a good time talking to Claire. I find out that she is new to the school this year and that she has yet to meet many people. I had experience with this first hand as well. Our school is very clique-y and it is hard to find a place if you hadn't had one since the first day of freshman year.

I sit with Claire again at lunch, and she keeps me company the rest of the day. We have a lot of interesting conversations, and I invite her to sit with Elias and I more often. I think he will like her.

That afternoon, however, my mom has to drive me to physical therapy alone. Luckily, I am perfectly comfortable with Sam and Lili, so besides Mom grumbling about having to drop me off and pick me up, everything is perfectly fine.

"How was your day at school today?" Lili asks me while I am staring intently at my toes, willing them to complete the toe yoga exercises I've been assigned.

"Good!" I respond, not wanting to elaborate for fear I will lose my focus and have to start over.

"I know that Elias was sick today, did you hang out with anybody new?"

"I actually did! This girl in my calculus class named Claire, she was really nice!" I answer excitedly.

"That's so cool, Abby! I'm really relieved that you've made another friend," Lili admits.

I slightly scoff to myself, it's not like I was completely friendless before today, I just didn't really feel like focusing my attention on meeting new people. I had Elias after all. But really, I see this as an achievement for me as well.

Lili continues as I keep counting my toe lifts in my head. "Elias is not going to be as happy though," she jokes.

I laugh at her comment. "You're right, he's not going to be nearly as cheerful."

Lili giggles as well. "Abbyyyyy! How could you replace me this quickly?? I thought I was your best friend!" She imitates Elias perfectly, sending me into a fit of hysterics.

I lose where I am in my exercises, but I can't help it. Her impression is so spot on! That will almost definitely be his reaction after the weekend.

"Ha! That was one hundred percent accurate! I will report back to you on Monday on what his reaction is, but I'm sure you are accurate," I say, tears now streaming down my face from laughing so hard.

"Thank you, Abby, I would greatly appreciate that," Lili confirms, still chuckling as well.

On the ride home from physical therapy, I tell my Mom about my new friend Claire as well, and she expresses the same emotions as Lili did.

"Oh! Abby, that's wonderful! I was hoping you would talk to someone new today! Was she nice?" Mom exclaims, taking her usual motherly stance.

"No Mom, she kicked me out of my wheelchair and laughed in my face, but I decided to befriend her anyway," I say sarcastically.

Mom rolls her eyes at the road, but I know they are directed at me. "Okay, okay I get it, stupid question. But she was kind, right? Like she didn't make any comment about your situation?"

I realize that she is genuinely concerned, so I make my answer more serious this time.

"Yes, Mom, she was perfectly caring and polite. Everything was fine, I don't want you to worry, not everybody treats me like Natalie and her group do."

She lets out a large sigh. "Thank goodness! Well that's good then, isn't it?"

"Yeah it is! Claire seems really cool, and I think that Elias will like her too, that way we can expand our group a little bit," I beam.

"That's awesome, honey!"

When I get home I shoot a quick text to Elias.

Abby : How are you feeling?

He responds quickly, clearly not being very far away from his phone.

Elias : Much better already, thank you :) How was school today? Did I miss anything?

Abby : Not much, we did have to do partner work in calc though.

Elias : Ohhh no way! I'm so sorry I wasn't there, who did you partner with?

Abby : This girl in our class named Claire, she was really sweet, I think you will like her!

Elias : The girl with the purple hair?

Abby : That's the one

Elias : Oh, okay then, I see I was very easily replaced, I didn't realize I was so disposable to you, Abby >:(

I laugh loudly at the message, causing Mom to give me a funny look. I ignore it, but lower the level of my giggles. Lili and I were right, he acted all offended just as we thought he would! And we got this reaction before I even saw him in person on Monday. I'll have to tell Lili as soon as I see her next.

I decide to play along with Elias in my answer to his text.

Abby : Oh no! You're still my best friend, I promise! How can I possibly get you to forgive me?

Elias : Hmmmm... I'm gonna go easy on you and let it go. Just this once though, do not betray me like this again

Abby : Alright I promise I will never betray you again, but doesn't you not coming to school in the first place count as a betrayal against me?

Elias : .... no comment

chapter 25:

"Daisy, stay where you are! Don't move, please!" I call out.

She's back again, but this time it's a memory that is not mine. I am in some sort of desert, surrounded by red sand and cactus plants. The sky is a picturesque blue, and there is not a single cloud in sight.

We are standing high up off the ground, near the edge of a jagged cliff that plummets down into the orange canyon below.

I am standing a few feet back from the edge, but Daisy is walking ahead of me, getting closer and closer to the sharp drop that lies ahead of us.

She is wearing the same outfit she was wearing on that *night. Her flowing white dress billows behind her, floating up in the air when there is even the slightest gust of wind.*

Her auburn curls fall perfectly onto her shoulders, sharply contrasting her colorless clothes.

Daisy still has her back to me as she glides further away from me, and nearer to danger.

"Daisy! Please!" I plead, louder this time. But she doesn't make any indication that she's heard me, and I do not slow her down at all.

"Daisy, don't! Come back to me Daisy! Don't go, stay here, please!" I yell, becoming more and more frantic with each passing second.

In my head, I know that logically this isn't the real Daisy. Daisy isn't here anymore. But my heart is reaching out to her. I can't lose her again, I need to keep her safe.

Daisy still doesn't answer my cries, but when she reaches the end of the rock we are standing on, she finally turns around to face me.

As her face comes into view, I am perplexed to see that she is showing no emotions of fear. Instead, her lips are pulled up into a smile and she looks unnaturally calm.

What are you doing? *I want to shout. But I cannot seem to make the words form in my mouth.*

My feet are firmly planted into the ground. I want to run to her, but I avoid doing so as I am afraid I may scare her away.

So I just stand still, staring right into Daisy's eyes. She still looks so placid, so peaceful, and I wonder how she can be doing that. Doesn't she know what could happen?

We stay like that for what feels like an eternity, neither one of us daring to make a move towards the other.

"Daisy," I finally manage to utter, but it is strangled and comes out sounding more like a hiccup. It is only then that I realized my face is coated in a salty substance. I am crying.

As soon as I notice this, my silent tears turn into full on sobs. I beg Daisy to stay. Shout to her over and over again. But her face remains perfectly content. She looks like a statue. So stoney, so emotionless. And when I finally look into her eyes, I am not shocked to find nothing behind them.

There is tense silence for a moment, as I finally try to reign in my feelings. I wipe my eyes with the palms of my hands, but when I look back up with more clarity, Daisy is gone.

My wailing starts back up again, and I sprint to the edge of the cliff, looking over into the abyss below.

She is still falling when I see her. Daisy has leaned off of the ridge and is suspended in the air, looking like she is floating down in slow motion.

Her clean dress pools around her body, and her hair is whipping up in the air, creating an almost beautiful image.

But now her face is not nearly as tranquil as it was before. The chilling smile was no longer there, replaced by a worried frown, and her eyes are terrified.

She seems to notice me crouching over the edge, reaching an arm out towards her, as a flash of recognition moves through her face.

One of her hands reaches up, grabbing at my figure above her, trying to grasp onto me. But she keeps falling. Down, down, down. "Abby!" she yelps at last. It's a heart wrenching, gut twisting cry out for help.

I want to do something so badly, but there is no way that I can.

"Daisy!" I shout one last time before she disappears into the darkness that awaits her.

I close my eyes, shaking my head, trying to rid myself of the events I just witnessed.

When I open them again I am back in my own room.

Breathing heavy and my shirt soaked with sweat. Far away from

the desert, far away from the cliff, far away from Daisy.

It wasn't real, I think to myself. *It was just a dream.*

But as I lift my hand to touch my face, I feel the entirely

authentic teardrops on my cheeks.

chapter 26:

"Alright class! Before you leave this afternoon I have an announcement for all of the juniors!" Mrs. Rose declares.

The few sophomores and seniors in my seventh period science class groan, clearly not happy to be left out of whatever is going on.

I turn to Elias next to me and raise my eyebrows at him. *Do you know what's going on?* I silently convey.

He shrugs, which I guess means he has no clue what the surprise announcement is, much like me.

"All 11th grade students will have the opportunity to go on a ski trip with their peers at the end of November. It's an annual tradition at Stonebrook High School, so I hope most of you decide to attend. There are financial aid options if needed, and I am about to hand out a permission slip for you and your parents to sign!" Mrs. Rose ends her short statement and begins to walk around the room, handing out sheets of paper to anyone who wants them.

I had forgotten all about the annual junior ski trip. It was definitely something that students looked forward to at my school, but I had completely let it slip my mind lately. I have wanted to go on that vacation forever, but I'm not sure that it is even going to be possible this year.

There is a loud cheer that comes from the class in excitement, but I just look at Elias, worried.

There is no way he would be up for going on a *ski trip* of all things. Not after what happened to Delilah.

When he peers over at me, he picks up on my concerns right away, and disappointment creeps onto his face. "I'm sorry, Abby," he starts. "But I really don't think I can go, I just don't think I can do it," he admits guiltily.

"Oh come on Elias, please?" I press. He looks like he might just change his mind if I can convince him. "I can't ski either! We can just chill in the hotel together. We can sit by the fire, play games, read books?"

His eyes meet mine, and I watch him go over the advantages and disadvantages of going, but I think I've gotten him loosened up to the idea.

Finally he breaks out into a grin that spreads across his entire face. "Fine," he groans. "I guess that does sound kind of fun."

He sounds reluctant, but I can tell that he is secretly very very excited, he's just trying to downplay it.

"Yay!" I exclaim, throwing myself into his chest to give him a hug. "You won't regret it, I promise!" I giggle in joy.

Mrs. Rose finally strides up to our desk.

"Abigail, Elias, do you both want the information sheet and permission slip?" she inquires.

"Yep!" I smile, and she hands me two papers. I give one over to Elias. "Thank you," I say to him, causing him to chuckle.

"No problem, Bennett."

Claire has been absent from school the past couple of days, so I haven't been able to introduce her to Elias yet. She has been gone getting her wisdom teeth out, but I am ecstatic to see that she is back today.

I notice her lilac hair stick out in the front of the classroom as soon as I sit down, and am immediately joyful to get to see her again.

I still have a few minutes before school starts, and Elias isn't present yet, so I call her name and wave her over to my desk.

She hops up, excited for someone to talk to, and rushes over to me, stopping in front of my chair and crouching next to the table.

"Abby!" she beams. "How are you?"

My response is bubbly, despite it still being early in the morning. "I'm doing good, Claire! How about you?"

"I'm okay as well, a little bit tired. If it wasn't 7am I would be doing a whole lot better," she jokes.

"I have to say, I am in total agreement with you there," I confess.

Before our conversation can continue, I spot Elias over Claire's shoulder, trotting towards me with that unnaturally large grin he always seems to have handy.

When we make eye contact, his face lights up, and he speeds up, jogging towards us now.

"Bennett!" he greets loudly, causing a few unwanted looks from other classmates.

I just glare at him in response, but he seems to get it now that I am not seriously mad, because he ignores my eyes and continues on his merry way.

Claire stays quiet as he arrives at our table and perches in his usual chair.

Elias says something first, choosing to scooch closer to me and wrap his arm around my shoulders humorously. "Abigail," he starts, leaning into me and making himself as goofy as ever. It makes me giggle. "Aren't you going to introduce me to our new friend here?"

Instead of answering right away, I lightly shove him off of me and place him back upright. "Are you good now?" I ask, and even though he makes a pouty face, he nods. "Alright then! Elias, this is Claire, and Claire, this is Elias." I gesture to the both of them, even though there is no one else near us that I could be referring to.

Polite grins are exchanged between them and it is awkward for a moment before conversation starts up again.

"I love your hair!" Elias compliments, and this seems to brighten the mood a little bit.

"Thank you!" Claire gushes. "I dyed it a couple of months ago and it is staying in much better than expected," she comments.

"Woah, that's weird, I don't know if I've ever had hair dye last that long," Elias recognizes.

This causes me to jutt in. "I'm sorry, you've colored your hair?"

He rolls his eyes as if he did not want a big deal to be made out of this information. "Yes, Abby. I've dyed my hair before."

I laugh at his reluctance. "Okay I have about a thousand questions, the main ones being how old were you and what color was it?"

"I was eleven years old and I colored my entire head bright blue," he admits.

Both Claire and I are amused now.

"And I'm guessing from your reaction that the results were not optimal?" Claire suggests.

"They were not," he confesses. "But that's the end of this discussion, okay?"

"Nope, not done yet!" I tease.

"We demand to see a picture of eleven year old Elias with blue hair!" Claire adds.

However, before we get to look at anything, the bell rings, meaning it is time for class to start.

"Thank God," Elias mutters under his breath.

"Don't think you're off the hook yet, Elias!" Claire calls over her shoulder as she skips back to her table, and I nod in consensus.

"Abbbbyyyyy," Elias whines, giving me his classic "puppy eyes" look.

I ruffle his hair with my hand. "Oh, Buddy," I say, faking sympathy. "You've brought this upon yourself!"

That day at lunch, Claire sits with Elias and I in the courtyard.

I am sitting in the middle of the two of them, with Elias on my left and Claire on my right.

About halfway through the break, we start talking about the upcoming junior ski trip. Claire is going as well, which makes me happy, but she says she thinks she will be on the mountain most of the time, so I probably won't see her as much as I would hope.

"Have you guys looked at the permission slip yet?" Claire asks the two of us.

My mouth is currently full of food, so Elias answers first.

"I haven't examined it closely, why?" he inquires.

"Oh! There's just a section where we have to pick our roommates, and I was wondering if you guys had thought about it yet," she responds.

I hadn't thought about it until right now, but my guess is we have to choose someone of the same gender, so Elias and I rooming together is probably not an option.

Luckily, I have recently made a new friend. "Would you want to be my roommate, Claire?" I request.

She grins, "That's what I was going to ask you!"

I beam back. "Great! We've got that sorted then!"

I am happy to have figured out the situation so quickly, but when I look back to my left, I realize that a certain boy is a little bit less joyful.

"Abby!" he scoffs, feigning offense. "I can't believe you would choose Claire over me! You've barely known each other for all of two minutes and you're already leaving me in the dust!"

"Don't you worry, Elias. We will still have plenty of time to hangout, I promise," I play along.

"But it won't be the same," he frowns. "Who am I supposed to share a room with? You guys are my only friends," he cries.

I roll my eyes. "Oh stop being so dramatic, I'm sure you'll be able to find someone."

He sticks his tongue out at me. "Fine, but I am expecting your undivided attention during the days," he huffs.

"I'll try not to steal her for the entire time, but I make no promises," Claire interjects.

Elias gasps, causing us two girls to double over in laughter.

"Not funny! You two are mean!" he says, but I can tell he too is holding in a chuckle.

The four weeks left until the trip become two, and the permission slips were due to our guidance counselors. Claire and I both put each other down for roommates, and Elias chose to ask one of the guys he knows from some club he was in last year.

Even though it's still a couple of weeks away, you can feel the excitement building among the junior students with every interaction.

So, naturally, almost all of Elias and I's discussions somehow drift to how we will be spending our time in the lodge, if we aren't doing any skiing or snowboarding. We come up with a few ideas: board games, reading, watching movies, and drinking a ton of hot chocolate.

All of this meaning, of course, that it is no surprise when on one of our drives back from physical therapy, our conversation returns to this exact topic.

"Ok, Abby, we need ideas," he begins, keeping his eyes on the road.

I am confused by his statement. "For what?"

"For what we're going to be doing for a whole three days in an empty lodge," he says, like it's obvious.

"Haven't we already talked about this subject enough?" I sigh, exasperated.

"No! No we have not!" he insists. "We've come up with a few activities, but nothing solid so far!"

"So what do you want me to do? Do we really need a step by step plan?"

"Well, no. But we do need an idea of any stuff we have to bring with us, right?" he suggests.

"Okay, okay fine! But we have two weeks!"

He shakes his head in mock disappointment. "Oh, Abby. Sweet, sweet, Abby. Those two weeks are going to go by so fast, and soon you're going to be wondering how time passed by so quickly. And guess what, when that happens you're going to wish we had come up with a plan sooner," he says adamantly.

"You can think that, but I don't happen to agree," I argue.

He acts annoyed but I see the smirk he is trying to hide. "Oh, yeah? And what do you think we should do?"

"I believe that we should just not think about it until we leave, and then we can figure all of this out when we get there."

Elias is a planner, I, however, am not.

His mouth drops open in shock, but he still doesn't look at me, too focused on driving.

"Abigail!" he gawks. "I can't believe you!"

We come to a stop at a red light, and he finally turns to me, smiling from ear to ear, clearly amused with himself.

"Hey! Eyes on the road!" I holler, pointing to the street in front of us.

"But I'm at a red light!" he protests.

"Eyes. On. The. Road."

He does his little nose scrunch thing but complies all the same, staring at the dark grey pole overhead.

We're both quiet for a second, before he tries to sneak another glance at me, thinking I won't pay him any attention.

However, it doesn't escape my notice, and I am the one to scrunch up my nose this time. He lets out a roar of laughter as I reach my hand out to poke his cheek, pushing his face back so that he is looking straight ahead again.

The light turns green right in time, and Elias presses on the gas pedal, sending us forward.

I secretly watch his face for a while, tracing his side profile while he stays focused on the street. His curly caramel hair, his perfectly round nose, his bright inescapable smile. All of it, just so Elias to me.

He turns his head quickly, just enough time to meet my eyes and give me a wink, before facing ahead again, like nothing happened.

This small, sweet, movement jolts something in my head, lets loose an intrusive, but not unpleasant, thought.

I like Elias Smith.

I should feel embarrassed by this realization. I should be metaphorically running as fast as I can in the other direction. I should be terrified of ruining the only good thing in my life right now.

But I'm not.

I feel safe and comforted by my emotions.

I like Elias Smith.

It feels so good to be saying those words in my head. It's like they have been there forever, but were waiting anxiously to be set free.

I keep repeating those four words over and over in my head, completely forgetting about my surroundings.

I realize with a start that we are already back at my house. I don't know how long we have been sitting here, but Elias still hasn't made any effort to get out of the car.

There is a flutter in my stomach as I turn to face him, expecting to meet his emerald green eyes. Thinking that if he looked into mine, he would surely sense that something was going on.

Instead I encounter an unusual sight. Elias is looking down into his lap, picking at a stray piece of thread on the hem of his T-shirt. He seems distant, like he is being consumed by his thoughts.

"Elias?" I say softly, and his eyes finally dart up to meet mine.

He seems to be debating a decision in his head for a second, before raising the rest of his body up from being hunched over.

"Abby," he decides. "I have a question for you."

"What is it?" I implore.

My heart is pounding. I hope I know what it is, but it feels impossible. There is no way he can read my mind. No way for him to know how I feel right now.

"I was just wondering if you wanted to hang out again sometime soon?" he asks apprehensively.

The question itself isn't very abnormal, but his nervous tone makes the butterflies in my stomach do backflips. There is only one reason why he would be acting like this. "Of course, was there something else?"

His cheeks flush bright red, which is a rare occurrence. His usual confident attitude is gone, as he continues to stutter, trying to figure out the right words to use.

Just ask me, Elias. I will say yes in a heartbeat. You just have to ask.

"Well, I was thinking...that this time it could be like an actual date?" Although his words don't quite form a question, the lilt at the end of his sentence suggests that it is. The butterflies in my stomach are doing full out gymnastics routines now.

How did he know?

But his expression suggests that he doesn't have any clue.
He still looks terrified and I can guess the reasons why.

I give him an affectionate smile. A gesture to show that I
am okay, and he doesn't need to worry at all. "I would love that."

His ears perk up, and my energetic, smiley Elias is back.
He seems even happier than before though. The largest grin I
have ever seen covers the entire bottom half of his face, and his
eyes twinkle in the sunlight coming through the windshield.

He looks so joyful, so relieved, like he just set down a five
hundred pound weight he had been carrying for weeks.

Once he seems to collect himself, he leans over the center
console and gives me one of his great, big bear hugs.

His arms engulf me and I am smushed into his chest.

This makes my new pet butterflies go wild again, but I
don't mind, not at all.

chapter 27:

Although I was afraid of something happening, my relationship with Elias doesn't change one bit after our conversation in the car.

Our usual back and forth banter hasn't changed, and I am so grateful for that.

Two days later, I am exiting my fourth period classroom and making my way down the winding hallways toward the courtyard, ready for lunch.

I can't wait to see Elias and Claire. The past few days we have been eating together as a group, and it is so refreshing to finally be building a new group of friends.

I pass all of my usual landmarks. The rows of lockers, the wall of windows, the set of bathrooms. I am almost to my freedom when I wind up passing Natalie's locker. Unlike most days, however, this time I don't just get to glide by.

Natalie is standing in the open door of her small space, but the usual posse that surrounds her at all times is nowhere to be seen.

I don't think Natalie is paying me any attention, but when I try to pass by her, she grabs the arm of my wheelchair, stopping me in my tracks.

"Abigail!" she says sweetly, but it is not so kind as much as it is sickening.

"Natalie," I note, trying to retain my cold exterior.

She pauses for a moment, seemingly confused by my attitude. That's the thing about Natalie, if you don't respond the way she's expecting you to, it baffles her. Every-time.

"Did you need something?" I ask, with no hint of enthusiasm. I cannot show her any emotion, or she will use it to benefit her. I'm sure of it.

My question gives her time to recollect herself, and her next sentence has the same honeyed tone to it. "Well, you see

Abigail, I was wondering if you wanted to go to the movies with my friends and I sometime-"

I start to decline before she even finishes her sentence. This may have worked on me a month ago, but I know that I don't want to be Natalie's friend anymore. She's mean, and toxic, and exactly the kind of person I am leaving behind this year.

But she cuts me off just as I did to her, narrowing her eyes and getting rid of her flawless pleasant facade. "And before you say no, be aware that this is your only chance Abigail. I'm willing to let you back into the group again, but this is a one time opportunity."

I have to hold in a scoff so I don't look rude. I don't care if this is my last chance, it won't change anything. But this fact doesn't stop me from being suspicious.

"And why are you only offering this now, after months of ignoring me?" I interrogate.

She seems satisfied that I'm engaging with her. "Oh! I don't think I was ignoring you Abigail! Simply giving you some distance to figure things out."

We both know that this is a lie but neither of us says anything about it.

"Oh come on Abby!" she exclaims, getting frustrated that I'm not complying. For some reason, she really wants to convince me to come to this movie night. "This is your chance to be popular again."

Up until then, I was set on not going. Until she said that word. *Popular.* That used to be my life. That used to be the only thing that mattered to me for so long.

And for some unknown reason, I find myself agreeing to go.

Her fraudulent smile returns quickly. "Great! I'll text you the details!" she chirps, and then skips down the hallway in the opposite direction.

What have I just gotten myself into.

It's late that night, around 11pm when I get a message from Elias. I am ready to go to bed, considering the social drama I had to endure today made me pretty tired, but I of course, stay up for a while longer to text with him.

Elias : We need a plan

Abby : I thought that we already discussed this! We do NOT need a plan yet!

Elias : No! Not about the trip! We need a plan for our upcoming date...

Abby : Oh my goodness yes, you're right this time

Elias : This time? Abby, I'm always right.

Abby : Whatever you say :)

Elias : I'm just going to ignore that. Anyway, I was thinking we could just come up with a date and time, and I can plan the rest.

Abby : As a surprise??

Elias : Yep :)

Abby : YAYYYYYY

Elias : Geez, I guess I know the way to your heart...

Abby : :)

Elias : I can pick you up and everything so that it all remains a mystery to you

Abby : I have to tell you Elias Smith, you are doing great so far!

Elias : Thank you, I appreciate that

Abby : So, when were you thinking?

Elias : This Saturday around, let's say 7?

Abby : Sounds like a plan :) You better have one heck of a date planned Smith

Elias : When have I ever let you down?

I may be playing a little bit hard to get with him, but I am positively sure that whatever Elias has planned, I will enjoy it. Honestly, that boy can ask me to do anything and I will have fun, as long as it is with him.

Feeling perfectly content, I set my phone down and fall asleep within seconds.

It's Saturday morning when I get my first text from Natalie in months. I'm sitting down eating breakfast and daydreaming about my date later tonight when my phone vibrates, signaling I am getting a message from someone. I check it right away, thinking it is something from Elias, but it's not what I am hoping for.

Natalie : Movie is tonight at 8. We'll meet you outside the entrance of the theater. You better be coming.

Shoot. Shoot shoot shoot. I can't do tonight. I can't just cancel on Elias. He's been working so hard planning this special night for us, and I desperately want to go out with him. Nevermind the fact that he would never forgive me.

But Natalie has made the situation very clear. This is my only chance. My one opportunity to be a part of my old group again. To have more friends. To have things go back to the way they were before the accident.

I mean, it's not like I'm completely abandoning Elias. It's just for one night, and then once we start officially dating, he'll be a part of the pack as well. The best of both worlds. I could be popular again, and take Elias and Claire with me.

A big part of me knows this is a bad idea, but I shove that doubt down.

Abby : I'll be there.

The next text I send is unexplainable. I somehow decide to lie to Elias. I convince myself that this is for the good of all of us. That I'm not making a selfish, impulsive decision. I stupidly tell myself that I'm not making the worst decision of my life.

Abby : Hey Elias, I'm so sorry but I think I'm going to have to cancel tonight. My mom is insisting on a family game night, and she's not budging :(

As soon as I send it I feel guilty and want to take it back, but it's too late for that now. He responds almost immediately, saying that it's okay and we'll find another time. He tries to sound casual, but I know that I've truly hurt him.

He'll benefit from this too, it's just one time, and then he'll thank me for this. I can have everything back to the way it was.

"Hey, Mom, can you drive me to the movie theater later tonight?"

She looks up at me from her laptop, where she is currently checking Facebook. "What time?"

I think about it for a moment, calculating the timing in my head. "Well the movie starts at eight, so probably around seven fifteen?"

Mom quickly pulls open the calendar app on her phone to make sure she doesn't have any prior commitments. I assume she has confirmed it when she responds, "Sure! Are you going with Elias or Claire?"

Oh no. I was hoping she wouldn't ask. "Neither actually."

Her face contorts from confusion as she runs through my short list of friends in her mind. She seems to come up empty. "Who are you going with then?"

I hesitate for a moment, not wanting Mom to get angry at me. "Natalie and some of her friends," I say, trying to sound nonchalant.

She averts her eyes back down to her laptop, clearly mad but trying not to lose it.

"And why would you want to hang out with her?" Her voice is strained and irritated. She is not happy with me. At all.

"I don't know, Mom! She invited me so I said yes. Is this really such a big deal?"

She lets out a long sigh. "It's not, Abby. I guess it's just unclear why you would ever want to hang out with those girls again, after the way they've treated you since the accident."

She sounds disappointed in me, which is almost worse than her actually yelling at me.

I can't look at her anymore, for fear of being overcome with guilt, so I lower my eyes to my hands, and start picking at my fingernails.

The room is silent for a moment, a cloud of tension hanging in the air between us.

"Fine," she finally says. "It's your choice, but just be careful, alright?"

I lift my gaze to meet hers. "I will, I promise."

She gives me a tight smile and returns to her computer.

It'll be okay Abby, everything will be fine. You just need to make it through tonight, and then everything will be perfect.

Mom drops me off outside the theater around seven thirty, which is a little bit earlier than I was hoping but I'm not going to complain, especially not after our argument earlier. As I watch her car pull away from the curb, I sit near one of the benches surrounding a fountain. The same place that I sat just a few weeks ago when Elias and I were here.

This time, though, it's much darker and cooler. Being well into November, the sun is setting very early, and frigid temperatures plague the night, sending shivers down my spine. The fountain is no longer spouting water, as it has been turned off for the winter.

I am regretting not bringing a jacket.

I text Natalie to let her know where I am, and quietly hope that her and the other girls arrive soon.

I scroll through the different apps on my phone as I wait anxiously, trying to avoid the awkward stares of other people on their way to the movies.

"Poor girl, she must be freezing!"

"Why doesn't she just go inside?"

Because I was told to meet Natalie out here. And I am not going to start tonight off by disobeying her only instruction.

Natalie can be nitpicky about the details, and I do not want her to be upset from the first moment she spots me.

She told me to wait outside, so I will wait outside.

I glance up at the time on my phone. 7:55pm.

I rub my hands together, trying to get them to warm up. The time doesn't mean anything, they're probably just taking their time getting here. I mean, I was the one who was early after all.

But the minutes keep passing by.

8 o'clock. No sign of anyone. It's fine though, people run late all the time.

8:15pm. I check Natalie's instagram for any signs on her story of where they are. Nothing.

8:30pm. By now I'm nearly positive, they're not coming.

I was set up. This is all just a sick joke to them. And I have no doubt that Natalie orchestrated all of it.

I knew this would happen. Deep down I knew this was a bad idea. Why did I ever go along with it?

I could be sitting at some fancy restaurant, or in some fun place with Elias right now, but instead, I'm all alone out here in the cold.

Tears blur my vision as I try to open my messages app, looking through my contacts until I reach the desired one. *Mom.*

Abby : Hey, Mom? Can you pick me up?

I don't want to sound as pathetic as I do, but honestly, I'm beyond that at this point. I don't care anymore.

I am so grateful when I get an immediate response.

Mama : On my way

Although I am eternally grateful, this message only serves to turn my previously hushed sniffles into full on sobs. Of course she's coming to get me. Because she's amazing. I don't deserve my mom. I don't deserve her kindness after the way I've treated her today, but she gives it to me anyway.

I turn my phone off and take a peek at my surroundings, hoping that if I focus on something else, the tears might slow down. I don't want to look like a complete mess in public. I'm already getting enough attention for sitting out here in the cold for an hour.

My fingers are becoming numb, so I hold them up to my mouth, breathing warm air into them in an attempt to provide some heat.

Just fifteen minutes and I can go home.

I can't wait to crawl into bed and forget tonight ever happened.

Once my crying has nearly stopped and I am finally able to see clearly again, I watch the cars driving past me on the road in front of the theater. I need to keep my mind off of the cold, so I watch the license plates, noting each of the different states I see.

California, Colorado, Texas, Florida, Indiana, Illinois…

Elias.

Elias?!

Crap.

Elias is here.

Why is he here? He's not supposed to be here. But he is.

He's walking towards me, chatting with his dad.

Both of them are so close to me. And I'm not supposed to be here either. I'm supposed to be at home, playing games with the rest of my family.

Luckily they don't seem to have spotted me yet, so I do my best to stay invisible. I avoid eye contact, I cover my head by resting it on my hand, I try to look insanely interested in my phone. But there's only so much you can do when you are in a wheelchair and also happen to be the only person sitting outside in these freezing temperatures.

"Abby, hey!" Elias exclaims, jogging over to greet me. Dr. Smith continues past me to the ticket counter, leaving the two of us alone.

"Hi, Elias!" I say, trying not to sound mortified.

He looks around me for a second, checking for another person that should be accompanying me, but when he comes up empty, he turns back to me.

And then I see it hit him. The conversation we had earlier. I'm supposed to be at home, not at the movies.

"Wait, what are you doing here? I thought it was family game night?" he asks. He's not interrogating me though, he still believes that I will have a reasonable explanation for me being here.

I don't answer him, instead I stare at the pavement. He's going to be so angry with me. I don't know if I can stand it.

But I have to. I can't lie to him again.

He crouches down so he can see my eyes again. "Abby?"

I take a deep breath. "I may not have been telling you the whole truth."

"What do you mean?"

"I'm so sorry Elias, you have to know that I feel so so bad."

"Abby, you're scaring me, what is it?"

I rip the band-aid off. "There was never any family event. I cancelled on you because Natalie asked me to come see a movie with her tonight."

He stays silent. The same emotion is present in his eyes as the one in my Mom's look earlier. Disappointment.

But it hurts so much more coming from Elias, because Elias put so much trust in me, and I betrayed him.

"But you have to believe me Elias, I am so so sorry. I promise you I will never do anything like this again. I really want to be with you, please," I stumble, tears threatening to spill out of my eyes once again.

I am so relieved to hear him speak, but his voice comes out cold and distant, sending my heart into panic. "So let me get this straight. You ditched me, on the night of our first date that I had extensively planned, to get together with some of your old popular friends who have been bullying you this entire school year?"

"I know, it's terrible but I thought I was doing the right thing. Please, Elias, let me make it up to you," I beg.

I stare deep into his eyes but there is nothing besides hurt behind them. "And let me guess, they never showed?"

I slowly shake my head, hot tears flooding my face.

"You know what, Abby? I'm done with this. I'll never be good enough for you, will I?"

"No! That's not it, I swear! Elias, please," I choke.

"No! You'll always just run back to Natalie and her crew! You say you don't care about them, but that's all you want, Abby! To be popular again. And that is just not me." he shouts.

Everything stills around us.

I messed everything up. I always mess everything up. Why did I ever talk to Natalie? I should have just shut her down right away, then none of this would have happened.

"I'm sorry," I whimper one last time.

"Yeah, alright. I'll see you later, Abigail," he says, defeated. He leaves and goes to join his dad by the doors. Leaving me behind, a disastrous heap.

I hear a small honk from the street, and see Mom's car waiting for me.

I'm still crying when I get in the passenger seat, but neither of us say anything until I start talking.

"You can say 'I told you so' if you want."

Her voice is soft and sympathetic. "And why would I feel the need to do that?"

"Because you did. Tell me so, I mean." This makes her laugh lightly, before turning all Mom mode on me again.

"I feel like you've been punished enough tonight, Abby."

"So, you saw what happened with Elias?" I ask apprehensively.

She exhales. "From beginning to end."

"I messed up big time, Mom. And I feel so bad about it. How do I fix it?" I ramble.

Her answer is simple. "I'm not sure you can, sweetie."

This sends me over the edge. "What am I supposed to do then? I can't lose one of the best friends I've ever had." My voice keeps breaking, and I sound so sad and helpless, reflecting my inner emotions.

There is quiet for a moment. I can hear the faint song playing on the radio, the cars passing us by on the street, my rough, jagged breathing.

Mom ponders her solution carefully, wanting her guidance to be helpful to me, while also being realistic.

"Give him a little bit of time," she advises.

I understand the reason why I should give Elias some space, but how on Earth am I supposed to survive that time? All of the physical therapy, school days, even the ski trip! They all involve him. So what am I going to do?

And that's not even including my biggest fear. "What if he never forgives me?"

My mom removes her gaze from the road for a minute and gives me a sympathetic smile. She reaches her right hand out to me and places it carefully on my cheek.

"He will eventually Abigail. You guys are such great friends, and I can't imagine this will keep you guys apart for long. Just let him get his head straight, okay?"

I nod solemnly.

She puts her hand back on the wheel and focuses on the street.

"I know you probably don't want this advice, but try to remember who your true friends are, Abby. I know you regret what happened, and I don't blame you for wanting to trust Natalie again, but I think you knew in your heart that it wasn't right. Is that a fair judgement for me to make?"

I think back on the past couple of days. She's right. I had doubts the entire time, I just pushed them down until they were unnoticeable.

I simply nod my head once again, thinking that less is more in this situation.

Mom notices my response and comments, "You should follow your heart, sweetie, and it will lead you down the right path next time."

It's exactly the kind of cliche guidance that I had been hearing my whole life, but it never really resonated with me until this moment.

I am so weak and defeated that I lay my head on the seatbelt and end up falling asleep before we even reach home.

chapter 28:

The next day, I don't even bother getting out of bed. It is a weekend anyway, so I decide to just lay by myself for hours, occasionally drifting in and out of sleep. Mom and Dad come into my room a few times to check on me, but I'm assuming they agreed it was a good idea to leave me alone for a while.

I never even open my phone, thinking that it would probably be better if I don't see anything from Natalie or the other populars on social media.

I don't eat any breakfast or lunch but once it gets to be about 5pm, I finally feel hungry and ready to eat some food. Still exhausted, I make the decision to just wait until dinner.

In the meantime, I stare at the ceiling of my bedroom. It is plain white, nothing hung up on it, but I trace any lines and cracks with my eyes, following them like vines winding above my bed.

My interesting scanning is interrupted by a small knock on the door. I think it must be Mom or Dad again, probably coming to ask if I want any sustenance, but am proven wrong as the door slowly opens, and a small eleven year old boy peaks around the edge, looking for me.

"Abby?" he whispers lightly, trying not to wake me if I did happen to still be asleep.

"Right here," I clarify, doing a tiny wave of my right hand in the air.

The blonde haired kid shuts the door softly behind him and runs over to my bed. He's still wearing a white and red soccer uniform, meaning he most likely had a game earlier that I missed.

I scoot over to the edge of my mattress, making room for Alex to hop on next to me. He sits cross legged facing me, concern evident in his eyes. I must really look terrible for an eleven year old to notice. But then again, Alex can be very perceptive when he wants to. So maybe I'm not as much of a mess as I think I am right now. One can only hope.

"What's wrong? Are you okay?" he inquires.

I ruffle his hair affectionately. "Yeah, buddy, I'm alright. Just a little bit down is all."

He frowns. "Are you sure? You seem pretty upset to me."

"I'm sure, Alex," I reassure him. "You don't have to worry about me. I'll be back up and about tomorrow."

He nods but still seems unsure. I can tell he's not going to push it any further though.

We stay there in a peaceful silence for a moment, before he surprises me by jumping over to my side of the bed and tackling me in a warm hug. It immediately lifts my mood, and takes my mind off of Natalie and Elias for a second, which is honestly such a relief.

"Aww! Thank you, Alex!" I chuckle.

He giggles excitedly as well before releasing me and sitting back on his heels.

A little lightbulb seems to go off in his head, causing him to remember something from earlier. "Oh!" he exclaims. "Dad and I got you something on the way back from my soccer game earlier, can I go get it?"

I give him the go ahead and he dashes out of my room and back downstairs. He leaves the door open, showing that he will be back in no time.

Less than a minute later, Alex arrives back in my doorway holding something behind his back. I try to lean around him to see what it is, but he swivels every-time I move, blocking the mystery object from my view.

"Close your eyes and hold out your hands," he instructs.

I do as he requests, but shortly after I put my hands in front of me, I pull them back again and open my eyes.

"Wait a minute, this won't be something gross like a tarantula or slime, right?" I confirm, just to cover all of my bases.

He playfully scoffs. "Really, Abby? Do you not trust me?"

I raise my eyebrows at him. "No I do not. Who knows what sort of mischief you get up to in your free time?"

He scrunches up his nose and I exaggerate a sigh, giving in.

"Fine, but if it does end up being something bad I'm going to be mad at you," I glare.

He just shrugs, which is not very encouraging, but I go along with it anyway.

I hesitantly hold out my hands and shut my eyes for the second time, and this time I don't pull them back until I am told to do so.

Alex drops something crinkly into my palms, and when he says to, I open my eyes to see three different packs of candy, ranging from M&Ms to gummy worms to Twizzlers.

After the emotional turmoil I have been through today, his gesture brings tears to my eyes.

"This is so sweet, I really appreciate it, Alex," I thank him. He steps away from the bed and shrugs, clearly not wanting the attention, but still smiles to himself, proud of his work.

"I just hope that it makes you feel a little better," he says sheepishly.

"It really does, I promise," I reply sincerely.

Our bonding is interrupted as Mom glides in, ready to help me downstairs for dinner. Alex ducks around the door as soon as our mom comes in, but I'm happy for any time I get to spend with him, especially when he's being as pleasant as he is today.

By the time Monday rolls around, I am no more prepared to face everybody than I was on Saturday night. I try to go through the day unnoticed, but it's hard to avoid everybody, especially Elias.

We still sit next to each other in some of our classes, but he makes a point to face away from me the entire time, and only speaks to me when required by the teacher.

At one point during calculus, I tap his shoulder to try to get him to look at me. He ignores me, so I try a few more times.

Eventually I give up and just apologize profusely to his back. I get no response.

Over the first half of the day, I probably send Elias fifty texts, each saying how sorry I am and begging him to forgive me. He does read all of the messages, but I never hear so much as a single word back from him.

During all of my passing periods I try to keep my distance from Natalie or any of her friends, but I can still hear them whispering and sniggering behind my back.

Look at her, she looks absolutely terrible.

Do you think she actually showed up on Saturday?

I would say yes, otherwise I don't think she would look so exhausted today.

You're probably right. Gosh, I can't believe Natalie's plan actually worked. Can you imagine being that desperate?

I don't even want to think about it.

I don't even have the energy to let their words hurt me. I am tired of being Natalie's little puppet, and I am not going to stand for it anymore.

Overall, my day is going horribly, and I'm not particularly looking forward to lunch break either. Surely Elias and Claire will band together, leaving me out. And even if they don't and Elias goes off somewhere by himself, it won't be the same without him.

So here I am, slowly rolling my wheelchair out into the open air, prepared for the worst. As the bright sun hits my eyes, I take a moment to adjust to my surroundings. Once everything becomes clear, I scan the layout of the courtyard. I check our normal lunch spot first, but only see Claire sitting there, already unpacking her lunch. She sees me notice her and waves me over with a bright smile.

I make my way over to her, still apprehensive about her position on me at the moment, but from first glance, she doesn't look upset or mad at me at all. That's a good sign.

As I'm wheeling over to the bench Claire is sitting on, I also get a glimpse of Elias. He's sitting as far away from Claire as possible, all the way on the other side of the yard. He doesn't look up to meet my gaze, but instead stares at a textbook he has opened in his lap.

When I finally reach Claire, she greets me with a cheerful "Hello!" and a warm grin that lightens my day, even if it is only a little bit.

I beam back at her, but I don't think it's very convincing because her sunny expression becomes filled with worry in a split second.

She words her next question carefully, as if stepping on eggshells. "I notice that Elias isn't sitting over here today, is something wrong between the two of you?"

I look back across the courtyard at him, but he is still not looking up.

I sigh loudly, letting my smile fade away. "I did something that made him really upset at me, with good reason, and I keep trying to apologize to him but he won't stop avoiding me. Which I do get, but I'm still exhausted regardless."

Claire looks over to Elias as well, examining his demeanor.

"That really sucks, are you alright?"

"I'm fine, I'm just scared about him," I confess.

"He's got to forgive you at some point, right?" she assures me.

"I'm not so sure Claire. I really messed up."

"What happened?" she asks, but then quickly adds on, "You don't have to answer, I'm just curious."

I explain everything that happened last week to her. The talks with Natalie, the text messages with Elias, and the way Friday night played out. Claire nods pensively every once in a while, but stays quiet for the most part.

"I know I should've just gone with Elias that night, and I should've never trusted Natalie in the first place, it was just so hard to think of the right thing in the moment. I was blinded by the idea of having just one aspect of my old life back," I finish.

"Abby, that's not all your fault," Claire soothes.

"You're being really nice, but I can't see any way to spin this in that direction. Everything was my decision, and I chose wrong."

"If my life was totally thrown off the rails, I would want to hold on to something as well," she sympathizes. "It makes perfect sense, and Elias will come around to see that eventually as well."

I give her a weak but genuine smile. "Thank you, Claire. I really appreciate your support."

She leans over and gives me a long hug. "It's no problem, Abby. I've got your back!"

Maybe Claire is right, and everything will be okay eventually. I really, really hope so.

At the end of the week, the previously anticipated but now dreaded junior ski trip rolls around. Luckily, I am set to room with Claire, so I don't have to worry about getting to know someone new, but I have no idea what I am supposed to be doing during the few days we are there.

Elias still isn't talking to me, and Claire, although apologetic, is still planning on skiing the slopes all day. So I have nothing to do and no one to talk to.

The first day of the trip, I reluctantly get out of bed early and eat breakfast with Claire before she heads out to ski, and then end up going back upstairs as soon as she leaves.

I stay in my scratchy hotel room bed all day, completing some homework and watching a few episodes of a show on Netflix. Without Elias, I have nothing else to do.

Claire comes back into our room around 4pm, and when asked why I hadn't left my bed, I simply grumble and turn away.

"Abby," Claire pushes. "Please come downstairs with me? We can stay just the two of us or we can hang out with some of the people I skied with today?"

I try to stall for a little bit. "Who did you ski with?"

"Oh! Just a few people I met literally today," she says, leaving out some crucial details, but I'm guessing I probably wouldn't know them even if she told me their names.

"Now, come onnnn," she groans while pulling me out of the covers and towards the edge of the bed.

I finally agree to leave with her, but make no promises that I will stay for more than a few minutes. She takes the compromise, and together we ride the elevator down to the lobby.

When we checked into the hotel last night, I didn't pay much attention to my surroundings, but I now realize how beautiful the lodge is.

There's a small restaurant to the right down a hallway from the reception desk, and on the other side is a luxurious lounging area, where I can see multiple students from our grade already hanging out.

There are four couches set in the middle of the open room, all facing towards each other in a square. Each wall surrounding the large area has a crackling fireplace, burning brightly and beckoning me with their warmth. There are also multiple gigantic armchairs in front of each fire, creating a very cozy feel to the space.

The whole place has a very mountain lodge feel to it, which I guess makes sense considering we are currently in the mountains.

Many kids are in the area of the couch square, socializing, and few people are scattered elsewhere, leaving the sides of the room practically empty.

Claire immediately makes a beeline for the middle of the room, and I follow behind her like a lost puppy, letting her take the lead.

Once we reach our destination, she starts chatting to a guy who I do not know but she must've met earlier today, and a girl that I think I recognize from my English class.

I sit on the outside of the conversation, quietly listening in and responding only when asked a direct question. Everybody is perfectly polite, I just don't exactly feel like actively participating at the moment.

Eventually, about ten minutes into the interaction, I drift away from the main social circle, and find myself next to one of the fires on the exterior of the room.

I position my wheelchair right in front of it, and let myself close my eyes for a moment and be consumed by the heat.

My peace is short lived, however, as I hear someone clear their throat behind me.

I slowly turn around to look at the large, cushy chairs behind me, and spot Elias sitting in one of them, staring at me. His eyes are hard to read, and I can't tell what emotions he is feeling right now.

"I'm so sorry. I didn't-I didn't realize that anyone was h-here. I'll leave," I stutter, already preparing to leave for one of the other fireplaces. I do not need to impose myself on him anymore, I have to accept that he will hopefully forgive me on his own time. He simply nods and does not make any eye contact with me.

I'm nearly past his chair when I hear him whisper a few words. I think it's mostly to himself, but something in me is not letting me leave before making sure.

I stop abruptly. "What was that? I couldn't hear you, Elias."

"Wait," he says a little louder this time.

I have to say, although I hoped for him to say something along those lines, I had pretty much given up. I am shocked, but there is no way I am going to run away now.

"Okay," I respond simply, not wanting to say anything to cause him to take back his decision.

I move myself so that I am back in front of the fire again, but this time with my back to it, making it so I am sitting directly in front of his knees.

We are both silent for a long time, and unlike many of the other times we've been together, the air between us is tense and uncomfortable. I shift my weight in my wheelchair a few times, nerves winning over the rest of my body.

"Abigail." His voice startles me.

"Hold on," I interject. "Before you say anything, I just want to say again I'm so so sorry about everything I did. And I know I don't deserve your forgiveness because you've been nothing but kind to me and I totally betrayed your trust but I *miss* you, Elias. It's only been a week and I can't stand the way our relationship is right now. I'm so upset all of the time and I just want this to be over, please," I beg.

The old Elias starts to peek out from behind the cloud of anger. His eyes go soft and a small smile creeps onto his face.

"What I was about to say, before you so rudely interrupted, was that I feel the same way."

And as soon as I hear those words leave his mouth, a surge of happiness and relief stronger than anything I've ever felt before hits me.

"You're serious?" I ask incredulously, still not quite believing that this isn't some sad joke.

"I'm serious," he beams. "I want us to be on good terms, and I trust that you won't do anything like that ever again."

"I won't, I promise!" I cry. "I will never ditch you again or do anything to hurt you for that matter."

We are both grinning like crazy people now, but there is no one else in a close enough proximity to us to notice.

"So then, you're saying that I'm forgiven?" I confirm.

"I'm saying that you're pretty darn close," he nods.

"Oh thank goodness," I breathe before closing the gap between us and pulling Elias into a long affectionate hug.

He gratefully accepts my gesture, and tugs me even deeper into his chest, clearly just as relieved as I am to have this all over. I know I still have some work to do before I'm completely in the clear, but all I can think about at the moment is how over the moon I am to be back on good terms with him.

I let out a breathy laugh. "I'm so happy right now."

His voice vibrates into my shoulder when he speaks. "I am too, Abby. So happy."

I stay with him for the rest of the night, catching up on all of the things that we missed in the past week, talking about school, family, friends, everything. We fall right back into our old rhythm, telling sarcastic jokes and laughing every few seconds.

He carries me out of my wheelchair so that I can sit with him in the large arm chair, and we stay curled up together until the chaperones declare lights out and we have to trek back upstairs.

While I walk with Claire back up to our room, she continuously shoots me sly grins and raised eyebrows, like she knows something I don't.

We walk into our room, and the heavy hotel door slams behind us, sealing us into privacy.

"Okay, what the heck was that all about?" I ask.

She feigns innocence. "What was what all about?"

I try again, this time being a little clearer. "All of those theatrics in the hallway! What are you smirking about?"

"Oh! All of *that*," says Claire while hopping onto her bed. She sits cross legged on the edge of the mattress, staring at me intently. "You guys are just so cute together," she gushes.

Blood rushes to my cheeks, tinting them a bright red.

"What do you mean, Claire? We're not dating, you know that," I blurt out.

"Well *obviously* I know that, but it's only a matter of time. It's clear that the two of you like each other."

I didn't think it was possible, but I become even more embarrassed by the second. I can't even deny her, because she knows Elias and I's dynamic well, and she would see right through me. Plus, my body is betraying me at the moment, my flushed cheeks and sweaty hands not exactly helping my case.

I let out a deep breath. "Alright fine, you're right," I groan.

"Yes! Yes! I knew it! Ha!" Claire bubbles while bouncing up and down with excitement. "I totally saw that coming but I've been waiting forever for you to finally tell me!"

I roll my eyes but still can't stop the grin that creeps up onto my face.

"Okay, okay, you caught me!" I giggle. "But you can't tell anybody yet, alright? I still need to figure things out with him."

Claire fist pumps in the air and skips off to the bathroom to get ready for bed. "Fine, just don't forget to invite me to the wedding!" she yells over her shoulder, making me chuckle.

chapter 29:

The morning after my conversation with Elias is the first time in a week I am actually excited to get on with my day. I joyfully get out of bed, brush my teeth, and put on a comfy outfit for the day. Claire watches me happily, following my wheelchair around our small room, and helping me get ready faster.

We bound down to breakfast around 8:30am. The lodge we are staying at provides a free breakfast buffet for everyone, which is situated in a large, open space, that I assume to be a conference room when not being used for food.

We glide through the wide open double doors and I am met with a wave of enthusiasm as I spot Elias already in the room, sitting at a table for three people.

"Elias!" Claire calls.

He lifts his head and waves us over to him eagerly.

"Hey guys!" he exclaims. "I saved both of you a seat!"

Claire and I sit down next to each other across from Elias. I push one of the plastic seats to the side and opt to stay in my wheelchair for the meal. Elias doesn't have any food yet, so I'm guessing he was waiting for us to come downstairs.

On the back wall of the room, there are multiple tables lined up with all sorts of different foods on them. There are eggs, toast, sausages, bagels, waffles, pancakes, cereal, and any other breakfast food you can imagine. I wasn't hungry before I got in here, but now that all of that deliciousness is right in front of me, my stomach starts growling like crazy.

Elias must notice me staring at the buffet because he chuckles and says, "You guys must be hungry, shall we go get something to eat?"

I nod ferociously, as does Claire, so the three of us trek over to the food and grab plates. I heap mine full of all the food I can fit without things falling off, and Elias offers to help me by carrying it back to the table. I reluctantly hand my plate of paradise over to him, but demand that he give it back as soon as we are back to our seats.

He laughs and places my food down carefully in front of me, making sure not to tip anything over. Claire is still getting her breakfast, but I'm too hungry to wait, so Elias and I start eating. He has grabbed just as much food as me, and seeing another similarity between us sends a warm feeling through my body.

Our table is silent, as we are both stuffing our faces full of too much food to talk. Claire trots over soon after we begin, and I can't help but notice she has barely taken anything.

I give her an odd look, as if to say *It's an all you can eat buffet, and all you have is one piece of toast and some scrambled eggs?*

"Oh, trust me, I wish I could fill myself up with carbs, but I actually have to go out and ski today, and I can't do that if I'm too full to move," she explains.

I stop eating for a moment to giggle. "Wow! I'm glad I just get to lay around all day, that sounds terrible!" I exaggerate.

"Oh! So terrible!" she agrees.

No more than five minutes later, Elias and I are about halfway through our plates, and Claire gets up to leave.

"Wait! No! You're going already?" I protest.

"Sorry, Abby! But I promised I would meet some people at 8:50, so I've got to head out," says Claire.

"Fine," I sigh. "Have fun!"

"Thanks!" And with that, Elias and I are left by ourselves.

We finish eating and head to the same part of the lodge that we were in last night. He carefully lifts me out of my wheelchair and places me in the corner of the large armchair, before sitting down across from me and pulling my legs up over his lap. It's a small gesture, but it makes the butterflies in my stomach reappear again, and start performing an acrobatic routine.

He reaches down to the ground and lifts a small backpack into his arms that I hadn't noticed before.

"Wait, what do you have?" I question.

"Oh, it's nothing," Elias claims, but he is still grinning like a child.

"Elias," I joke. "You'd better tell me before I grab that bag from you and figure it out myself."

"Okayyyy," he says, dragging out his word in reluctance.

He pulls out two leather sketchbooks and a tray of colored pencils. "We obviously don't have to do this, but I thought that it could be fun if we both drew each other. You know, just to have something to do?" he explains. I immediately love the idea.

"Yes! That sounds great!" I cheer, eager to get started. "I have to warn you though, I'm not a great artist."

"Neither am I! That's the fun part!" Elias laughs.

"Awesome!" I reach across our laps to grab one of the books from him. "So, is there a time limit or anything that I should be aware of?"

"I was thinking we could have an hour?" he suggests.

"An hour?!" I ask incredulously. "I was thinking it would be closer to ten minutes!"

"Well then, I guess that just leaves you more time to get *all* of the details right," he teases.

I playfully roll my eyes. "Mhm sure. I'm going to spend those extra fifty minutes drawing an incredibly detailed human sized dog next to you instead."

"A dog? Why a dog?" he chuckles.

"Because dogs are the only thing I *can* draw, okay? No judging!"

He lifts his hands up in surrender. "Okay, okay! I concede! You can draw all the dogs you want."

"Yay!" I cheer, glad to have won our fake argument.

Elias pulls out his phone and sets a one hour timer. "Alright Abigail Bennett, are you ready to have the most intense drawing contest of your lifetime?"

"Elias Smith, I am ready," I confirm.

"On your marks," he starts.

"Get set," I continue.

"Go!" And with that we are off!

I work really hard on my drawing. I start with the basic outline of a stick figure, but try to test my artistic abilities by actually spending time on the details, contrary to what I had decided earlier.

I add all of the intricacies of Elias's face. Focusing my drawing on his bright smile, his emerald eyes, his messy hair, until there is nothing left that I have missed.

I check the timer, and to my surprise, there are only five minutes left. Elias is still deeply engaged in his drawing, staring at the paper with such intensity, I wonder if he even remembers that I am here. He doesn't notice me watching him work, and as I do, I catch him sticking out his tongue while he is focusing. It's the cutest little action I've ever seen, and he probably doesn't even know that he's doing it.

The alarm sounds, and we both jerk out of our dazes.

He looks back up at me, eyes twinkling.

"Are you done?" he inquires.

"Of course I'm done, Mr. Smith. I am very serious about this competition, and I would never try to get extra time," I say, putting on a very serious voice and straightening my posture.

Elias, as usual, goes with my joke and plays along. "Ah, yes, of course Ms. Bennett. I apologize for questioning your commitment to this challenge. Please forgive me?"

"You are forgiven. Just make sure to never do it again," I conclude, letting my solemn exterior fall into a much sillier one. "Shall I show you mine first?" I suggest, fairly confident in my portrait of him.

He nods impatiently, clearly excited to see what I created.

I turn my masterpiece around to face him. He gazes at it for a moment before he decides to speak.

"No dogs?" he questions.

"No dogs," I concur.

He looks at it for a while longer.

"Abigail," he says after a moment. "That is genuinely amazing!"

I breathe a sigh of relief, glad that he likes it. "Really?"

"Yes, really! I absolutely love it."

I blush. "Are you sure? I mean, I know it's not technically flawless but I did my best to capture your essence and-"

"It's perfect," Elias reassures softly.

"Thank you," I say quietly, before handing the drawing over to him. He takes it and delicately puts it to the side as he showcases his own piece.

"Okay, um, here's mine," he says, shyly.

He flips the piece of paper around to face me, and his portrait puts mine to shame. My mouth drops open in shock.

It takes me a moment to say anything, for Elias's drawing is truly artwork. He drew my features with such care, such precision, that I almost can't believe it's me.

I playfully hit his legs. "Elias!" I accuse. "You said you couldn't draw!"

"Well, I can't really-" he tries but I interrupt quickly.

"Yes, yes you can. This is absolutely wonderful. I mean, I don't even know how you did this," I encourage.

Now it's his turn to be embarrassed. His cheeks flush pink, and match the shade mine were only a few minutes ago.

"It's truly amazing," I reiterate.

Things go silent between us for a moment. And although there are most likely other people around the lounge, I tune all of them out, only focusing on the two of us.

Things were lighthearted only minutes ago, but the mood between us has changed, and I can't pinpoint the exact moment it happened.

"Abby," Elias whispers, simply.

It is then that I notice, without a doubt, that our faces are closer together than they were before. I realize that our lips are only inches apart, but neither of us moves away.

"Elias," I say back.

Without warning, he places his hands on the sides of my head and pulls me forward to press his lips against mine.

Warmth radiates throughout my entire body. This is the moment I have been waiting for. The butterflies are back, and this time they represent pure joy. I feel an explosion of happiness inside and at this very moment everything in my world is perfect. I feel complete.

When he pulls away, he stares deep into my eyes.

We're both grinning from ear to ear, like children in a candy shop.

"I've been waiting to do that for a long time," he confesses.

"Me too," I breathe.

We lean back on the seat, legs still folded over each other, hearts pounding.

I can feel Elias working up the courage to say something, so I sit quietly and listen.

He looks back over to me, and I gaze right back at him, taking in all of his happiness, and creating a snapshot in my mind of the image to remember later.

He clears his throat. "Abigail Bennett, will you be my girlfriend?" he asks giddily.

I nod my head like a crazy woman. "Yes!" I beam.

My reward is that award-worthy Elias Smith smile, and it makes me lean in and kiss him again. I want to stay in this moment forever. It is the closest thing I've ever felt to flying. Soaring high above this lodge, this mountain, this planet, everything. It is the purest form of happiness I've ever known and it's magical.

As originally planned, I spend the rest of the ski trip with Elias. We eat meals together with Claire, but while she is gone during the day, he and I sit in the lodge doing all sorts of fun stuff. We play games (Elias is really bad at Uno, I don't know how, but I beat him every time), read books, talk, and simply bond.

When I tell Claire about everything that happened between Elias and me, including the kissing and girlfriend stuff, she goes absolutely crazy with excitement. I guess I should have expected as much from our biggest supporter, but she still manages to surpass any level of enthusiasm I predicted.

Claire won't stop making plans for future dates for us, and her eyes go all googly when she sees Elias and I do so much as hug. I decide to go along with it, giggling along with her and letting her have her fun for a little while.

The time to go home comes way too soon, and I wish I could stay up in the mountains with Elias and Claire forever, but sadly that isn't possible.

At 7am on Sunday, all of the students pile on to three coach buses designated to carry us back to the school, where our parents will be waiting for us.

We toss our luggage into the compartments below the bus, and rush to get the best seats possible.

While on the way here the bus was filled with excited chatter and laughter, the mood today is much more melancholy. It is clear that every student is already missing the freedom of our time away.

Although I sat next to Claire on the ride up, she is happy to forgo her seat for Elias, and moves to sit next to one of her new skiing buddies.

So Elias and I ride back home together. It's a four hour drive, and after waking up so early today, I am already exhausted. Most people are asleep by the time the bus gets moving, and others are talking in quiet, hushed voices, mindful of their tired peers.

Elias lets me take the window seat, and is very helpful with carrying me around in order to make the whole wheelchair deal a little easier for the teachers. They store my chair in a small compartment near the back of the bus, ready to grab in a hurry if needed.

Although I have no way of getting up or moving around, with Elias by my side, I do not feel trapped in any way. I feel safe.

We lean back in our seats as the bus travels down the winding mountain roads, both of us still subdued from lack of sleep.

Elias and I have a quiet conversation, whispering back and forth so that no one else can hear us.

Elias is telling me about some previous adventures he has had on buses like this one, specifically on his eighth grade Washington D.C. trip, while I rest my head on his shoulder.

"So everyone is absolutely exhausted on the bus, right? Because we've had a long day of running around D.C. and it's about 11pm by now. And our tour guide is standing up at the front of the bus droning on and on about our schedule for tomorrow but everyone is clearly zoned out and falling asleep."

He looks at me for guidance to continue so I nod. "Mhm, go on."

"The tour guide must've mentioned at some point that we were going to be visiting the capitol building the next day because all of a sudden she just blurted out, 'You know, I saw Bill Nye once at the capitol building' and that got people's attention.

"But then she had to deal with a hundred sleep deprived teenagers chanting 'BILL BILL BILL BILL' so I'm not sure that was any better."

Towards the end of his story, I find it harder and harder to keep my eyes open. They keep fluttering shut, and my mind is drifting in and out of sleep, blurring Elias's words together.

"Abby...Abby? Oh! You're asleep. I should stop talking now, huh? Well, goodnight I guess? Is it still goodnight even though it's morning? I don't know. I guess I should shut up now though. Talk to you later, okay? Okay," I hear Elias whisper, but I'm too far gone to even so much as chuckle in response.

chapter 30:

When I open my eyes again, I can tell immediately that I am not on the bus anymore. But I don't remember ever getting off. And I most certainly don't remember being back at home.

I glance around at my surroundings. I'm in our kitchen, but the usually crowded room is uncharacteristically empty.

My heartbeat quickens. This isn't right. This isn't home.

My brain tells me to stay put, worried that I'm in danger, but my feet carry me to the kitchen table anyway.

My feet? My feet! I'm walking normally. This must be a dream. It has to be, unless I've completed five more months of therapy without knowing it.

The realization that I'm in a dream comes with even more fear, as my legs continue to carry me to the table on the far side of the room.

My head swivels on my shoulders, looking for the person behind my disobeying feet, but still spot no one around me. Everything is still. Nothing is moving.

I reluctantly pull out my chair at the table, and take a seat, like I would normally do for family dinners.

I am still sitting at an empty table. Where is everybody?

I scan the room once more, and come up short. However, as I turn back to face forward, food has magically appeared at the table, as well as Mom, Dad, and Alex.

They're all grabbing food and eating with smiles on their faces, like they always do. I seem to be the only one with this sinking feeling in my stomach.

"How was your day, Abby?" Mom asks.

And although I still feel deeply uneasy, I answer her with a calm and even tone.

"It was good, I didn't do much." What I don't say is that I can't remember anything that I did. It's like there's a void in my memories that I can't reach.

The table is quiet for a while; the only sounds coming from the scraping of forks and knives on plates.

"So," my dad begins. "Are you all packed up for tomorrow?"

This confuses me. I don't belong in this odd alternate dream universe, and I definitely don't know where I am supposed to be going.

"What do you mean? What's tomorrow?" I clarify.

Alex, Mom, and Dad all start laughing in unison. It creeps me out and deepens the pit in my stomach.

"Always the jokester, Abby! You're going to jail, remember?" Mom says, oddly nonchalant.

My breathing becomes shallow and I can feel my heart pounding in my throat. "W-what do you m-mean? J-jail?" I stammer.

"Of course, Abby!" chimes Alex, eerily cheerful. "For killing Daisy! You sure are forgetful tonight." *He says it like a joke, but this is beyond serious to me.*

I'm in a nightmare.

They're still grinning alarmingly, completely devoid of emotion.

"No!" I yell. "I didn't kill her! It was an accident!" *My voice is panicked and frantic.*

They do nothing, they just sit there staring at me, eyes glossed over.

"It wasn't my fault! I didn't do anything, I swear!"

Still nothing.

"Guys! Help me, please! I didn't kill Daisy! It was an accident!"
Tears are flooding my cheeks now, spilling over my chin and onto my shirt.

"It was an accident! It was an accident! It was an accident!" I
repeat over and over again, but I can't tell if it's to convince my family or
myself.

"Abby!" I hear my name, but none of the creatures sitting in front
of me had opened their mouths.

My voice echoes around me. "It was an accident! It was an
accident! It was an accident!"

"Abby!" There it is again. It's not coming from here, it's coming
from somewhere far away. Although I think it's closer than the last time I
heard it.

"It was an accident! It was an accident! It was an accident!" I
scream over and over. I shut my eyes tight and cover my ears with my hands,
shaking my head.

"Abigail!" This time my name is sharper, right next to my ear, and when I open my eyes I am back on the bus.

Elias is close to my face, staring into my eyes, worry prevalent in his features.

At first, I am relieved. I'm safe again, away from the terrifying nightmare. But then I look past Elias's face, and at the rest of the students on the bus.

All of them are staring at me with looks of pity.

I question it for a second, but then register the way my cheeks feel wet and cold, my throat hoarse. I wasn't just dreaming, I was screaming and crying back in the real world as well.

Embarrassed, I look away from them and focus on the landscape blurring by the window.

I feel most of their eyes divert quickly, but one pair remains.

"Abby, are you alright?" Elias questions, concerned.

I simply shake my head, not trusting my voice to say anything without cracking.

He tugs me into a comforting hug, burying my head into his shoulder and stroking my back up and down. I break down crying again, quietly sobbing into his fuzzy sweater, but I have a feeling he doesn't mind.

He's whispering "It wasn't your fault," again and again into my ear and cradling my head close to his chest.

After a few moments, I am significantly calmer, and am now mostly worried about the embarrassment from freaking out in a bus full of people.

Because of this, I keep my head hidden in Elias's shoulder for a while after I stop the tears.

"Hey, Abby?" Elias whispers.

"Yeah?" I reply.

"Are you feeling better?"

"Yup," I confirm.

"Did you want to maybe sit up now?"

I knew this was coming. "Eliassss," I groan. "I don't want to look up, everyone is going to be staring at me!" I whine.

"You'll be fine, Abby. Trust me, I've done way more embarrassing things than this, and look at me! I'm fine!" he reassures.

"That's questionable," I mumble.

I feel his shoulders bounce as he laughs. "Okay, well you're going to be perfectly fine, I swear! Look! Everyone's already forgotten about it." he promises.

I slightly peer above Elias and take a glance at the seats around us, and for the most part he's right. People are back to doing what normal teenagers do. Talking, listening to music, sleeping, all things that don't involve gawking at me.

Phew. Well, things seem to be going well so far. I slowly move back from Elias, opting to lean against the back of the seat instead.

"See! Everything is all good, right?" he reiterates.

I nod, letting out a breathy sigh. "Elias, thank you for helping me out there, I really appreciate it."

And the look he gives me makes me melt. It's filled with so much care and love, that it makes my insides feel warm and my heart full. "Anytime, Abby, you know that."

When we get back to our school, I notice dozens of cars sitting in the parking lot, waiting to take their students home. I spot my mom's car immediately, and although I will miss the excitement of the ski trip, I am also glad to be home. This next week is our Thanksgiving break, so I'll get a lot of time to relax.

I am able to get off of the bus and grab my luggage in a relatively smooth fashion (mainly thanks to Elias), and he walks over to Mom's car with me.

As I get closer and closer to the vehicle, Mom sees me and steps out of the driver's seat, ready to greet me and help load my stuff.

She gives me a small wave and flashes me a welcoming smile, and I copy her actions. When I have almost reached her, Elias has to break off and walk in the direction of his own car.

"Alright, well I guess I'll see you later," he says.

"Yeah I guess so," I admit. "We definitely have to hang out over the break though!"

"Oh, for sure! I'll text you later, and we can plan something, sound good?" Elias asks animatedly.

"Yup! Sounds great!" I confirm.

We wave goodbye and he heads off to his car on the other side of the parking lot.

I travel the last few feet to Mom quickly, happy to see her again even though it's only been a few days.

"Abby!" she squeals while leaning down to give me a small embrace. "How was your trip? Was it amazing?"

"It was awesome! I had a lot of fun!" I answer while she picks up my bag and puts it in the trunk.

"I'm assuming everything between you and Elias is normal again?" she questions, noting the interaction she just witnessed.

"It is! He forgave me our first night at the lodge," I bubble.

"Okay, I want to hear all of the details, but let's get you in the car first," Mom states, and I agree.

However, when I try to move to the passenger side of the car, Mom guides me back over to the back seat.

"Actually, your dad and brother wanted to come with me to get you so you'll have to sit in the second row," she explains.

Dad and Alex are here! My whole family being here makes me even more delighted than I would have expected, but I guess I'm not used to being away from them.

When I am all settled in my seat, I look next to me and see that, indeed, Alex is in the car waiting for me. He's playing a game on his phone, but when he hears me plop down he turns it off and looks up.

"Abby!" he chimes. "Welcome home!"

"Thanks, Alex!" I reply.

My dad just turns around and smiles at me from the front seat, and I beam right back at him.

"So, honey, why don't you tell us all about your time in the mountains?" Mom suggests as she gracefully backs out of her parking spot.

While we drive home, I describe all of my memories of the trip to my family. All three of them listen intently, even Alex, who usually gets bored by now.

I tell them about how sad I was the first day there, how Elias forgave me by the fireplace, and how we spent the next few days hanging out together for all waking hours. I even tell them about how I am now officially his girlfriend!

When I say this, Alex threatens to beat Elias up if he ever hurts me. He then proves his point by punching and kicking in the air in front of his seat.

We have almost reached our house by the time I am done with all of the storytelling.

"It seems like you had a really nice time, Abby," notes my Dad.

"Yeah, I'm really glad," Mom agrees. "I have to admit, I was a little bit concerned that you would just be miserable the entire time."

"Mom!" I exclaim, exasperated. "I would have found some way to have fun, I have other friends you know!"

"I know, I know, it doesn't stop me from worrying though!" she defends.

My Dad chuckles and rubs Mom's shoulder as she pulls into our driveway.

"And that's what makes you a great mother," he soothes.

Alex and I both make loud gagging noises, making the whole car fill with laughter.

chapter 31:

5 months later...

"Okay I'm going to run through our checklist for the day to make sure we've got everything," Mom orders. I give her a thumbs up and she starts reading from her list.

"Get your dress back from the tailors?"

"Check."

"Shower and do your nail polish?"

"Check and check." I wiggle my fingers to prove my point.

"Hair and makeup?"

"Not done yet, but about to happen."

"And then we just have you getting all dressed up and ready!" she sighs, relieved.

"Sounds great! Let's do this!"

We're in the kitchen going through everything we need for tonight. *Prom.* The most important night of many high schoolers lives up until that point.

And tonight is an especially big deal for me.

I accomplished my goal of walking by prom. Actually *walking.* I can't believe I did it and am so proud of myself.

Now, don't get me wrong, I'm still very wobbly and I can't do much besides take a few steps, but I am so much farther on the path to recovery than I ever thought I would be. So, I'm grateful for any and all progress I've made.

I also fulfilled our idea of keeping it a secret from Elias. This *entire* time. Which was already very hard considering he was at physical therapy with me most of the time (I ended up having to schedule a few secret sessions with Lili to be ready in time), but got so much harder when we started dating.

There have been many close calls, but I made it until now, and I can't wait to surprise him later tonight.

But first, I've got to get ready.

Mom and I quickly move upstairs to her bathroom, where she wants to help me with my hairstyle and makeup.

Although I am very accustomed to making myself look good on my own by now, I let her take the lead, because I know she has always dreamed of this moment.

I sit in front of her large countertop and mirror while she shakes my hair out of the towel and starts brushing it out smoothly.

I sit patiently, watching Mom do her thing. We already have a plan for the way I want my hair to look, so all that's needed now is the execution.

She blow-drys it a little bit first, making sure my long golden hair is dry before she styles it into loose curls.

Once every piece of hair is perfectly in place, she pulls the front pieces of my hair up behind my head and pins them back, leaving a few strands framing my face.

"Ta-da!" Mom flourishes, stepping back to admire her work. It looks absolutely beautiful. My hair looks exactly the way

I dreamed it would ever since I was a little girl, and it's stunning. I almost can't believe I'm looking at my own head.

I've never liked school dances, but Prom was the big one that I always knew I could look forward to. When I was younger I would imagine myself looking like one of the princesses I dreamed of, and in this moment I do.

"Wow, Mom! It looks gorgeous! I can't believe you made my hair look this good! You're a miracle worker!" I compliment.

She laughs and swats her hand in the air as if to say "Oh, it was nothing!"

She sets everything with hairspray, and then moves on to makeup. The hair took about an hour, so we have an hour left until Elias gets here, giving us just enough time.

As Mom gets to work, I start playing our favorite songs from the Mamma Mia movies and the two of us hum along, even performing some dance moves when we remember them.

Mom puts every makeup item on me that you can imagine. And she does it perfectly, no smudging or unwanted lines anywhere. Concealer, foundation, blush, eyeshadow, eyeliner, mascara, and all of it looks so pretty and smooth.

Mom uses a light pink eyeshadow to match with my lilac dress, and creates a subtle and sweet makeup look, that isn't too much nor too little.

It, just like the hair, is absolute perfection.

I feel the most beautiful I ever have in my entire life.

I slip into my dress, now that I'm able to stand for short periods of time this is much easier, and stare at myself in the mirror.

I fell in love with this dress the first time I saw it. It's the most enchanting purple color, and has light lavender lacy flowers covering the bodice and cascading down the skirt. The upper part of the dress is held up by spaghetti straps, which is perfect so I don't get too hot while dancing, and the lower part of the dress poofs out a little bit, but not too much that it looks like some sort of eighteenth century design. It's exquisite.

Everything about it was just right, and Mom and I agreed that it was the one. I'm very excited for Elias to see it. I already know that his jaw is going to drop.

Mom delicately helps me put on my jewelry, a few golden bracelets, a necklace, and some earrings.

And right as we finish up, the doorbell rings.

I'm not quite ready to take on the staircase yet, so Mom and Dad help me downstairs like usual.

Once I am settled into my wheelchair at the bottom, I roll to the edge of the corner and get ready to stand up. I peek around the wall to see Elias waiting by the door, awkwardly looking at his surroundings. He's been over to my house a million times, but he still looks uncomfortable when he's not accompanied by me.

He is wearing a light grey suit with a pale purple tie to match my dress (I told him the color beforehand) and is carrying a corsage in his right hand.

I carefully get up from my chair, Mom and Dad close behind me, and take a deep breath. It's not that I'm necessarily nervous, it's just that the anticipation for this surprise has been building up for so long, and I want everything to go perfectly.

I round the corner slowly, taking small steps towards my date and looking down at my feet, watching them miraculously move.

I glance up just in time to watch as Elias's eyes land on me. And my prediction was right, his jaw drops comically wide open. He takes in my dress, my hair, my makeup, everything that Mom and I spent so long working on.

"Abby, you look beautiful," he marvels.

He hurries towards me to slide the flower onto my wrist, and kisses me lightly on my cheek, which is when he finally seems to notice the big difference about tonight.

I see the realization hit his eyes, which start glowing with pride. His stare darts down to my legs and then back up to my face.

"You're walking?" he confirms, not quite believing that his eyes aren't deceiving him.

"I'm walking," I smile.

"You're walking!" he gasps, amazed. "Abby! You're doing it!"

He lifts me up and spins me around in the air.

"I'm so proud of you!" he whoops.

I giggle at his excitement. This is exactly the reaction I was hoping for.

He sets me down gently and gazes deep into my eyes.

"When did you make this happen? How did you get all of this done without me knowing?" he asks sincerely.

"Well it was quite difficult to be honest," I joke. "You're basically with me 24/7!"

"I am, aren't I!" Elias chuckles.

I then go through the last few months, explaining all of the secret meetings with Sam and Lili and all of the extra exercises I had taken on without him knowing.

"You're incredible," Elias says when I finish.

"Thanks," I blush.

"Alright!" Mom interrupts. "I need photos before the two of you leave so stop being all cute and get over here!"

We take a ton of photos both inside and outside of my house, and Alex even comes to the front porch to pose with me.

We take a few pictures with me standing, but I get tired quickly and the rest end up being either in my wheelchair, or with Elias carrying me, the latter being insanely cute.

After what feels like a full length photoshoot, Elias and I climb into his car, waving goodbye to my parents.

As he stashes my wheelchair into the trunk, I catch a glimpse of something red and white in the corner of my eye. It's in the second row of seats, and upon closer inspection, looks like some sort of picnic blanket? There is also a dark brown woven basket that I assume goes together with the blanket.

Elias opens the driver's side door, and sits down next to me. I give him a questioning look.

"What's wrong, Abby?" he inquires, confused by my odd facial expression.

"Elias," I start. "Why is there a strange blanket and basket in the backseat?"

The concern in his face melts into a lopsided grin. "You weren't the only one with a surprise planned for tonight," he says mysteriously before pulling onto the road and starting to drive...in the opposite direction of the school.

chapter 32:

"Elias!" I laugh. "What do you have planned? Where are we going?"

His response doesn't clear anything up. "It's a surprise, Abby, and if I told you it would no longer remain surprising, therefore, I am not telling you."

"Okay, that's fine, but just to be clear, we're not going to prom?"

"Abby," he stares at me intently. "You've told me over and over again that you hate school dances."

"But I was excited for this one," I pout. "Because I was going with you."

"Aww, honey, you're so sweet!" He lifts my hand to his lips and kisses it. "But you're going to love this, I promise," Elias assures.

"What about Claire?" I ask. We were *supposed* to meet her at the school, but apparently that is no longer happening.

"This was actually her idea!" Elias exclaims. "I swear, everything is all taken care of."

I open my mouth.

"Including your parents," he adds.

I close my mouth again.

"Fine!" I give in after failing to come up with any more excuses. "I'll go along with your little plan!"

"Yay!" He pumps his fist in the air. "Thank you Abbyyy!"

I give him a playful glare but can't stop the smile that creeps onto my face.

"So you're really not going to tell me what we're doing?" I press.

"I'm really not going to tell you," Elias responds.

I huff and stare out the passenger window, looking for some sign of where we are going.

"We're having a picnic, aren't we?" I blurt.

He drops his mouth open in shock. "How did you know?!"

"Elias, there is a literal checkered blanket and a basket of food in the backseat," I laugh.

He makes a pouty face and scrunches his nose at me. "Fine, maybe I could've done a better job of hiding it, but I couldn't fit it in the trunk with your wheelchair."

I lean across the center console and kiss Elias's cheek. This makes a giddy smile pop onto his face. "Don't worry! I love the idea, and I am very proud of you for figuring this all out."

He gets a little bit embarrassed by my praise, and his cheeks tint a little bit pink.

"Anything for you, Bennett," he says bashfully.

We soon arrive at a beautiful park next to a lake and we set up a little picnic area in a secluded section of the grass. It isn't too crowded, so we are able to have a nice quiet area to ourselves.

Elias helps me sit down on the soft checkered blanket and moves to do the same. And there we are. Two teenagers dressed in their most formal clothes sitting on the ground in the middle of a public park. I giggle at the image.

Once we are both settled, Elias starts going through the picnic basket, pulling out all of the different foods he packed with him, giving me explanations as he goes.

He pauses with his hand still in the basket. "Just so you know, none of this is very special or anything like that. You know that I can't cook!" he jokes.

"I'm sure I will love it regardless," I encourage.

"Alrighty then! First up-" He pulls out two squares of tinfoil. "We have a couple of peanut butter and jelly sandwiches, because you bring them to lunch everyday so I know you love them."

"I do!" I agree enthusiastically.

He grins, proud of his accomplishment.

"I also brought some chips to eat on the side." He holds up a can of Pringles and a bag of Baked Lays.

"Then, we have some strawberries and blueberries, as a nice healthy snack," he lifts up a tupperware of fruit to show me. I nod.

"And finally, for the grand finale, we have an assortment of desserts; including homemade chocolate chip cookies from Delilah, some Twizzlers, and, of course, M&Ms!"

He finishes laying all of the food out into a spread on the blanket and looks up at me for approval.

"This is amazing Elias!" I praise. "I am genuinely proud of you for coming up with all of this. It's so thoughtful."

He lets out a sigh of relief. "I'm so glad you like it! I'm not going to lie, I was a little bit worried that you would be mad at me for ruining our prom."

"But you didn't ruin it! You just made it even better!" I propose.

"That was the goal!" he offers. "But I'm happy that I made it happen. I just want to give you the best night possible."

"And you are," I assure him.

I lean over to kiss him softly before sitting back again and eyeing all of the delicious looking food.

"Now, we should eat, I'm starving!" I insist.

But before I am able to get my sandwich unwrapped, Elias interrupts.

"Oh! And I also brought some drinks for us!" He rummages through the basket again and pulls out two cans of Sprite, my favorite.

"Gosh, you know me so well!" I gush. "This is all perfect!"

He gives me a grateful beam and then we both start to eat our food.

As predicted, everything tastes absolutely amazing and we have the best time just sitting and talking together.

Although it's not the image of the prom I've had in my head forever, it is even better than I ever imagined. This isn't even something I knew I wanted, but it is clearly making me happier than some silly high school dance would.

Old Abigail would have hated this. She would have laughed in Elias's face and gone to the dance anyway. After all, she would've probably been gunning for prom queen, and this whole romantic park date would not be on her agenda. But thank God I am not her anymore.

Thinking back to the beginning of this school year, so much in my life has clearly changed, but the thing that is most prevalent to me is that I am happier. I had no idea that I was unhappy in the first place, but looking back on it, I definitely was.

I was surrounded by toxic people and I was just like them. I was terrible to others, and although I have had a rough year, I'm so thrilled that I am no longer in that place.

I am close to people who actually love me, instead of those who just view me as a number.

"Abby?" Elias says, startling me out of my daze. "You good?"

I blink a few times as I zone back into the real world.

"Yup! I'm fine!" I reply.

"Are you sure? You seemed a little bit off for a second there," he suggests.

"Yeah, yeah, I'm okay. I was just thinking about how much has changed since the beginning of this school year," I confess.

He pulls me into his side and lets my head rest on his shoulder.

"Oh yeah? I guess you're right," he agrees. "I didn't even know you when we started Junior year," he gasps. "That's crazy!"

"I know, right? I feel like I've known you forever."

"You must've been so miserable before you met me," he says sarcastically.

I can tell that he is surprised when I actually agree with him. "That's literally what I was just thinking about."

"Abby, I was kidding, I know that you had friends and a busy life."

"That's accurate, but even though I didn't realize it at the time, I was never truly happy. I just acted like it on the surface. I was with a superficial friend group and I never stopped to think about how I actually felt. I was always just following Natalie and everything she desired. I had no idea what I actually wanted for myself." I admit.

Elias kisses the top of my head when I'm done speaking. "I'm really sorry, Abby. I know that you have had a really hard time this year, and I'm just so happy to be in your life now."

"Me too," I smile. "I just want you to know how much I love being with you, and how lucky I feel to get to spend time with you everyday."

"You feel lucky? Gosh, Abby! I'm the lucky one in this relationship! You are way out of my league!"

I sit up quickly. "No way! It's totally the other way around!"

He raises his eyebrows.

"Okay, fine! Let's just agree to disagree on this one," I concede.

Elias grins. "Sounds good to me!"

We are in silence for a moment as I lay my head back down on his shoulder and relax into him again.

I just have one last thing to mention. "Anyways, I also just want to say thank you for sticking with me through everything. I know that it hasn't been the easiest choice for you, but I want to let you know that I really appreciate it." Tears roll down my cheeks towards the end of my statement and Elias gently wipes them with his thumb.

"I will always stay with you, no matter what. I've got your back, Abby, there's no need to thank me for that," he responds sincerely. "It's what we do for the people we love," he adds.

"Well, I'm thanking you anyway because I know I can be a pain in the butt sometimes," I mumble.

Elias chuckles and I feel his shoulders jerk up and down. "That may be slightly true, but I'm still here, aren't I? Even after you broke my heart that one time?"

"Ugh, don't remind me!" I groan, burying my face into his shirt, causing him to laugh and pet the back of my head.

"Just know that I promise to continue supporting you as long as you do the same for me, as I have no doubt you will," Elias vows.

I lift my body up and hold my pinky finger out. "Pinky promise?"

He wraps his pinky around mine. "Pinky promise," he nods.

The sun has started to set around us in a brilliant show of pink, orange, and gold, so Elias pulls me into his lap and we snuggle up together. We watch as the sun slowly lowers itself closer and closer to the horizon until it is gone.

The days after prom blur by, after all, it's the last week of our Junior year. Teachers have started to slow down their lessons as we finish up our finals, and students are readying themselves for Senior year. That's crazy to me, it feels like just yesterday I was roaming these halls as a Freshman, and now we are about to be the oldest kids at Stonebrook High School.

Elias is helping me pack up all of the stuff from my locker, which was barely used this year anyway, when I remember the scene in the hallway at the beginning of this year. The one where Natalie and I tripped that poor little Freshman girl.

I feel an overwhelming sense of growth in myself. I am proud of how far I have come from that mean-girl personality I used to have.

There are not many people in the corridor right now, as we get to clean out our lockers during our last math classes, so it's just a few classes worth of students in the halls.

Luckily that means that the main reason I did not use my locker this year (Natalie's being two doors down from mine) is not going to be a problem for the moment.

Claire is here as well, but she is on the other side of the hall gathering her things.

I assist Elias in shoving magnets and photos into my backpack until the bell eventually rings, meaning time is up.

As we shut the door students flood out of the classroom doors and collect in the hallways, walking quickly to get to their next classes.

Claire walks over to join Elias and I. As we are about to get going, I spot a familiar face scurrying down the same path that she took the first week of school.

It's the strawberry haired girl. She has a slightly different haircut and looks a little bit older, but it's definitely her, the freshman that Natalie and I tripped in August.

"Hold on guys, there is something I have to do real quick," I tell Elias and Claire. They both nod, giving me the go-ahead, and I wheel my chair over to the small girl. Although, this time, I am shorter than her.

Even though I was hoping she had forgotten about me, she steps backwards a little bit, scared, when she sees me. She definitely remembers.

When I reach her, I plant a big smile on my face in the most non-threatening way I can manage and stick out my right hand.

"Hey there, I'm Abigail."

Printed in Great Britain
by Amazon

83274114R00231